# CERBAN

STARLIGHT MERMEN

STARLIGHT ALIEN MAIL ORDER BRIDES
BOOK 8

SKYE MACKINNON

Peryton Press

# CONTENTS


Glossary      9

Chapter 1      11
Chapter 2      19
Chapter 3      27
Chapter 4      35
Chapter 5      43
Chapter 6      53
Chapter 7      61
Chapter 8      69
Chapter 9      77
Chapter 10      85
Chapter 11      95
Chapter 12      103
Chapter 13      111
Chapter 14      119
Chapter 15      129
Chapter 16      139
Chapter 17      149
Chapter 18      161
Chapter 19      167
Chapter 20      177
Epilogue      183

Intergalactic Dating Agency      187
The Starlight Universe      188
About the Author      190
Also By      192

*To those who ban books.*
*You suck.*
*Get a life.*
*Read some smut.*
*Be happy.*

# GLOSSARY

**Eynhallow** – a city on Finfolkaheem

**Finfolkaheem** – planet of the finfolk

**Intergalactic Authority (IA)** – space police

**Intergalactic University (IGU)** – the best and biggest university in the galaxy

**Mooncrossing** – a year on Finfolkaheem

**Roussay** – a town on Finfolkaheem

**Span** – a week on Finfolkaheem

**Sunpass** – a day on Finfolkaheem

1

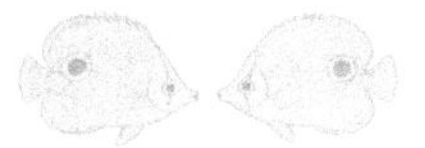

Maelis

Aliens were idiots. They came here all high and mighty, expecting us to bow to their superior technology, but deep down, they were idiots.

I waved at the back of the alien who'd interrupted my work to ask where Paul, the resort manager, was. Everyone knew that Tuesday was Paul's day off. And even if someone didn't, they could have asked someone in the central part of the island, not walk all the way out to my diving shack. As I said. Idiots.

I bet the alien had wanted to see if I was the unlucky woman to be his mate. They could tell by scent, or so I'd heard. I shuddered. Yuck. I didn't even want to think about the possibility. I wasn't racist – speciest? I just didn't want the complications of being with an alien from another galaxy.

The finmen were only the second species of alien I'd encountered, but they hadn't changed my mind about extraterrestrials. Not one bit. The excitement of working in a super-secret location, signing NDAs by the dozen, meeting men from other planets - it had quickly dissipated when it had turned into everyday life. This island was probably the most unusual place on Earth, yet to me, it was home, work and all I'd known for the past two years.

It was a crazy place. Bringing humans and aliens together wasn't a good idea, if you asked me, but nobody ever did. I was just here to entertain them with dives to the coral reefs or snorkelling trips along the coastline. It was the best-paid job I'd ever had, don't get me wrong, but some days, I would have given anything for a normal nine to five office job that didn't involve UFOs and multi-dicked aliens.

Maybe that was the reason for their superiority complex. Too much testosterone. If aliens had the same hormones as us. Despite being surrounded by them, I knew surprisingly little about their anatomy - except for the two dicks. That had filtered through the grapevine rather quickly. Although I wasn't sure if the current aliens, the finmen, were built that way. Only one human woman had been matched with one and she'd refused to tell.

Elise and her beau, a finman warrior called Fionn, had set off for Scotland last night. She wanted to show him where she'd grown up. I didn't know how she'd hide a seven foot, green-skinned hulk of a man who preferred walking around half-naked and who had growths that looked like seaweed all over his body. Paul said that some aliens had camouflage technology that enabled them to blend in among humans, but I'd not seen the finmen use that.

There were about twenty of them on the island, all of them huge, gorgeous and arrogant as fuck. At first, they'd stayed in their spaceship, with only four of them walking around freely. But that had changed when they'd all joined the Hot Tatties Dating Agency. They'd submitted their DNA profiles and questionnaires and were now waiting desperately to be matched to human women. But even though they were free to explore the island, they were under strict instructions to avoid all contact with female staff. One of them, their leader, had abducted Elise, which had left a constant fear with everyone that it might happen again. It was accepted that it was almost impossible for them to not be around human women at all – more than half the resort staff was female – but they weren't allowed to be alone with one of us.

I was happy with that arrangement. But soon, there would be new women brought here by the dating agency and everything would change.

Poor girls. I couldn't see the attraction myself. Yes, the finmen were pretty to look at, but they were *aliens*.

This island was a safe place for them to stroll around like they owned this planet, but who'd want to stay here forever? Human-alien couples would have to find somewhere to live where they weren't stared at - and where neither of them would end up being experimented on by the authorities. It all seemed very complicated.

There was only one finman who'd caught my eye. I didn't know his name, didn't know why he'd stood out to me, but whenever I saw him walk along the shore, water pearling on his pale green skin, I couldn't help but ogle.

And I had a good excuse to watch the beach. When I didn't have clients for diving or snorkelling lessons, I was the resident lifeguard. Right now, there were no human guests on the island. A group of women had landed on a neighbouring island, but instead of bringing them here as planned, Hot Tatties had decided to keep them there until they'd been matched with a finman - or another alien. Or maybe none at all. There was never a guarantee when it came to finding love. I knew all about that.

I focused back on my task of checking the diving equipment. I had one of my most random playlists blaring from the little Bluetooth speaker behind me. I should have turned it off; it kept distracting me. I'd been dancing to one of the songs earlier before I'd even realised that I'd stood up. Sometimes, music just took hold of me like that. But I should focus. I didn't know when I'd have my next guests to guide to my favourite place in the entire world: the ocean.

That was the best thing about living on the island. I was constantly surrounded by the smell and sound of the sea. It was in my blood.

It didn't take long to finish labelling all the equipment. A few items ended up on a pile for repairs, but most of it was in top condition. Hot Tatties had poured a shitload of money into this resort, and everything was high quality, including my diving shack. No matter how much I disliked the aliens, this job was the best I'd ever had. And the pay was more than I could spend.

It wasn't even midday, and I was more or less done with my work for the day. Technically, Paul was my boss, but he gave me free rein as long as everything got done. He wouldn't mind if I went for a dive during work hours. It was practice, I supposed. And I'd found mentions of an underwater cave on an old map of the island that I wanted to explore. I'd thought I'd seen all the caves in the island's vicinity, but I almost hoped I'd missed one. I loved the thrill of diving to a place very few had ever seen before.

I examined the map one last time, then put on my wetsuit and grabbed my equipment. For a moment, I wondered whether to take the camera, but at the last moment I took it with me. Yes, I'd filmed hundreds of hours of diving along the reef, but you never knew when you'd see a rare species of fish or something unpredictable below the waves.

When I stepped outside, I crashed into a wall of green alien. I jumped back with a shriek, almost dropping the diving cylinder. Green skin. Muscles as far as the eye could see. No clothes except for a leather wrap around his waist. Short black hair with an emerald tinge. Algae hanging from his shoulders, hips, legs. Webbing between his toes. And, strangest of all, gills at the side of his neck.

It was him. The guy I'd been ogling from afar. And he seemed even taller this close.

"I apologise," he said in a deep voice that reminded me of the depths of the ocean.

"No... I should have been more careful."

I almost had to crane my head to look up at him. He was smiling at me, exposing rows of sharp, pointy teeth. Definitely not human. His gaze swept down my body as if he was seeing me for the first time. Maybe he was. This was the closest we'd ever been to each other. I wished I hadn't put my wetsuit on. It didn't leave anything to the imagination. My hips were wide at the best of times, but in the wetsuit, they looked humongous.

I turned away from him, suddenly very self-conscious. "I have to go."

"What is that sound? Is that music?"

I had to focus hard to ignore the sound of my heart beating in my chest and instead listen to the song that had started playing on my little speaker. And of course it had to be a song that needed some explanation.

"Yes, it's music," I said simply, facing him again.

The alien smirked, as if aware that I was purposely taciturn. "If all Earth music is like this, I will start listening to it myself. She is singing strong words. Finding a new home. Readying to fight. Leading others. Tell me about it."

I sighed. I should have just left. But I couldn't. "It's called 'Stand up' by Cynthia Erivo. It features in a movie called *Harriet* about the Underground Railroad. She was an amazing person. A hero. But I don't have time to explain. Look it up if you want. I'm sure you can access our internet."

His smirk only grew wider as he studied me. Those sharp teeth made me think of a shark considering its prey. He wasn't supposed to be here, not when I was by myself.

"I'm going for a dive," I said firmly when he kept on staring at me. "Have a nice day."

Before I could change my mind, I tightened my grip on my scuba equipment and walked away from him, down to the beach.

"Careful, there's a storm coming," he called after me.

A storm? It was a beautiful day. A light breeze tousled the unruly strands of hair that had escaped my bun. The sun was high in the sky, heating up the sand. There was no storm coming. He just wanted attention.

I resisted the urge to look back.

# 2

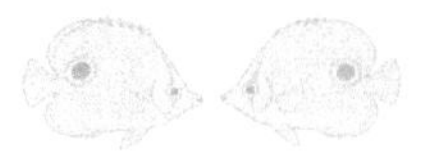

Cerban

I couldn't get her out of my mind. I was supposed to focus on the upcoming meeting with the Hot Tatties Dating Agency, but instead, my thoughts centred on the little Peritan... no, human. The agency had made it clear that we should use human terminology in order to fit in better with the locals. Peritans were humans and Peritus was Earth.

My brothers and I had already acquired a basic command of one of their languages, English, while travelling here, but now lessons were compulsory for all finmen on the island. Yes, we had translator implants that could do the job, but they weren't always completely accurate. Something always got lost in translation. I'd noticed that during our long journey to this planet. Not all the finmen on the Tidebound came from the same country as my clutch-brothers and I. Kelon, our former, now disgraced leader, had hired crew members from all over Finfolkaheem. There had been at least one violent argument born from a simple misunderstanding that could be put down to the implants not understanding the finer nuances of language and culture.

The accommodation building came into view, and I fastened my steps when I saw Rainse was on guard duty outside. My other clutch-brother, Fionn, was away with his mate, taking the Tidebound and half the crew with them. In the absence of the captain, the two of us were in charge. It was laughable. All three of us were simple guards. Yes, we had been trained as warriors, but Rainse was the only one who had seen real fighting action. That was before he'd been thrown out of the navy for arguing with his superiors. I couldn't help but grin. My clutch-brother had always had an issue with authority. And now he was one half of the authority. The irony was immense.

He raised a hand in greeting. "Ready for the meeting?"

It took me a moment to remember what meeting he was talking about. My head was full of the human female. And I didn't even know her name. Maybe Rainse knew. He always seemed to be chatting with humans.

"Not really. Why do we need yet another meeting?"

Rainse chuckled. "Because the first batch of test results is going to come in any sunpass now. The agency wants to make sure that this won't cause chaos among the finmen. Kelon's behaviour has made us look like unpredictable brutes. Pam and the others are worried the rest of us will behave similarly."

I growled softly. Kelon had betrayed us all when he'd kidnapped a human female who hadn't been matched to him. It had all had a happy end - she was mated to Fionn now and Kelon had been sent back to Finfolkaheem to be punished - but it had left a bad taste not just with the dating agency, but also the rest of us. We'd come to Earth to find mates with the help of a human-run dating agency, not to take females by force. Kelon was a stain on our reputation that would be hard to rub out.

The female danced into my mind again. Did she think that we were violent brutes? Was she scared of us?

She hadn't seemed scared, just irritated. She hadn't enjoyed my presence. If she'd known that I had been standing outside her building for a while, listening to her music, watching her sway to the rhythm, she would have been even more upset. Let's hope she never found out.

"Cerban?" Rainse looked at me strangely. "Are you alright?"

"Yes, just thinking. Do you know... never mind. Can you show me how to access Earth's outernet?"

"Internet?" He laughed. "It astounds me every time just how bad you are with technology."

I flicked his greenskin in response.

He flinched but kept laughing. "Yes, I can show you. What do you want to search for?"

"A song. A beautiful song about a female."

His smile faltered somewhat. "What are you up to, brother? You know we aren't supposed to be alone with females on the island, not until we have been matched by the agency."

"It's hard to avoid when so many of the staff are female," I grumbled. "Anyway, just show me how to access this internet."

"I will. *After* the meeting. I need you to focus. I don't want to feel like I'm the only one listening."

I checked my holoband. I had just enough time for a snack and a piss. No time to look up that song again or find out the female's name. Fuck. It would have to wait. I had to be a responsible adult male for once.

Rainse sniffed the air. "There's a storm coming."

"I know. Can't see it yet, but it's coming fast."

As was that damned meeting.

Pam looked perfectly put together as always. She was an older female, but she oozed authority. She was used to telling others what to do - especially males. In the absence of both Fionn and Paul, the human resort manager, we were joined by Eneda, a female I'd only met once before. I dimly remembered that she was responsible of the island's finances, or something similarly dull. She was younger than me, with thick eyeglasses hovering on the tip of her nose and hair the colour of seashells.

Rainse looked her up and down, then exchanged a look with me. Not his mate. I gave him a barely noticeable nod. Nor mine.

It had become a custom among finmen on the island. Whenever we met a human female, we would wonder, was this her? Had we finally found our mate? So far, Fionn had been the only one to be that lucky.

"What news?" Rainse asked after greetings and formalities.

Pam smiled widely. "We have finally heard from the lab after submitting all your finmen's DNA samples. They've been analysed and compared to the women's DNA markers that we have stored in our database. I got the results two hours ago." Her dramatic pause drove me crazy. Was this the moment I'd been waiting for? My greenskin tightened at the thought.

Next to me, Rainse had his fists balled. His gills were fluttering ever so softly.

"There are two matches," Pam continued. I stopped breathing. "Neither of the two women was part of the contingent we sent to the island, so it will take some time to contact them and bring them to you. But we will work as fast as we can, of course. We know how desperate you all are to meet your matches."

I almost growled at her. Couldn't she just give us all the information at once?

"Who are the two males?" I asked, forcing myself to keep my voice neutral.

Pam checked her notes. "Pli'th and Hournn. It is your choice if you tell them now or if you wait until the women are on their way."

"Hournn is away on the Tidebound," Rainse said. I didn't have to look at my clutch-brother to know of his disappointment. I felt it too. Yet another setback. Another spark of hope extinguished.

I took a deep breath. "I think we should wait until he's back and then tell them both at the same time."

Rainse nodded. "I agree. They will be frantic once they find out. Let's not risk the peace on the island until we know for sure that the two females are on an air vessel."

"Air... Ah, you mean a plane," Eneda said, speaking for the first time. "I tend to agree. Paul is back tomorrow and I'm sure he will want to organise some activities for the lucky couples, introducing them to each other slowly. I know you finmen will want to rush into it, but remember, these women don't know that aliens exist. It will be a shock to them. Elise handled it remarkably well, but we cannot expect everyone to behave like that. I certainly didn't."

She chuckled at the memory but didn't expand further.

Pam and Eneda continued to chat, but I couldn't focus on their conversation.

No mate for me.

When we had submitted our genetic samples, we'd been so full of hope. The Hot Tatties agency had a vast database of human females. Surely there had to be a match. And there had been, for three of us. But none for me.

For some reason, my mind wandered to the diving instructor again. Her smooth black hair that I wanted to run my fingers over, her beautiful brown eyes that seemed to sparkle around the pupil, her tiny body that would fit so perfectly against my own...

No. She was off limits. Pam and Paul had made it very clear that staff on the island, especially the females, were to have as little contact with us as possible. After what had happened with Kelon, we'd have to earn their trust again.

After the meeting, I'd get Rainse to play that song for me on the humans' internet. And then I would go for a swim in the storm. It wouldn't be long until it hit the island. And there was nothing better than surfing the frenzied current brought up by a storm.

# 3

Maelis

A school of foureye butterflyfish swam past me, diving and ducking around the corals. They had a dark spot surrounded by a white ring on their sides, resembling a huge eye, to confuse predators. I always loved seeing these nimble little fish, especially when they swam in pairs. They were one of the few fish to mate for life. Not many humans managed to do that.

I watched them for a while. It was such a relaxing sight, hundreds of fish hunting for food around the corrals, completely ignoring my presence. I was alone down here, yet I was also surrounded by life. I would have smiled contently if I didn't have the regulator in my mouth.

I had to pull myself away from the reef. My air cylinder wouldn't last forever. If I wanted to explore that cave, I couldn't linger. I had no idea how big that cave was, how much time I'd need to explore it. With one last look at a butterflyfish couple, I followed a crevasse that I knew would lead me to an underwater cliff. Somewhere in its towering wall was the cave. I'd dived there many times before. The cave entrance had to be covered by something for me to not have spotted it in the past. Maybe it had collapsed over time, and I was setting myself up for disappointment. But I wouldn't know without first diving there.

I felt it the moment I broke through the thermocline. I wore my full-length wetsuit and only my face was exposed to the water, but it was enough to feel the change in temperature. I always loved breaking through this invisible barrier. It felt like going on an adventure.

The cliff face looked smooth from afar, but once you got close you noticed just how cragged it was. The ocean current hadn't smoothed the volcanic rock and wouldn't for a long time. Small fish swam in and out of cracks and holes, while others were feeding on the algae that was painting the grey rocks green. I knew of a small cave further south, a tunnel that narrowed to an arm's width after only two metres, but the cave I was looking for had been described as something much bigger. Maybe I was about to discover the local version of La Catedral, a stunning underwater cave in the Canary Islands that I'd been lucky enough to visit last summer. I would be very surprised if it was that big, however. I'd been diving here for years. I would have stumbled across anything as magnificent.

I swam slowly to conserve both energy and air, descending ever deeper into the dark waters. When it got too dark, I turned on my torch, illuminating the cliff I was using as a guide. The fish surrounding me here were smaller and less colourful than the ones at the reef. A whitespotted eagle ray elegantly floated in the distance. They generally avoided divers, but I would make sure to keep a safe distance from its venomous tail spines. Keeping aware of what else was swimming in the sea was important in these waters. Sharks, rays, jellyfish all posed a risk - but one I was willing to take.

The water moved oddly, little surges that didn't match the usual rhythm of the tide. A storm brewing above; maybe the alien had been right. I dismissed it. I'd dived through worse. And I was only going deeper, where the effects of the storm would be barely noticeable.

A dark shadow on the cliff face caught my eye. I pointed my torch at it, half-expecting to see a cave entrance. No such luck. It was just an isolated algae patch, nothing more.

According to the old records I'd found, the cave should be somewhere here. The description had been vague, but I knew this island well enough to recognise the underwater features mentioned. It had to be in this area. I stopped my descent and scanned the craggy rocks with my torch. There was less algae growth down here where sunlight was becoming sparser. Thin veins of a darker sediment looked like they'd been painted onto the cliff. This was so very different from the busy, colourful coral reefs that I usually dived to, but no less beautiful in its own gloomy way.

Something sparkly caught my eye, a little further up the cliff and to my right. A few air bubbles rose to the surface, shimmering like little gems in the light of my torch. Something was producing them. There were too many to come from plants. Fish didn't create bubbles. Yet I doubted a dolphin or whale had squeezed into a gash in the cliff. And while some of the other resort staff liked snorkelling at the reef, I was the only diver on the island right now.

I followed the stream of bubbles to its source. The beam of my torch caught on a patch of algae that rippled strangely, not with the current but as if clinging to something that wasn't stone. I brushed at it with gloved fingers. To my surprise, the dark green veil parted, revealing a shadowed hollow just big enough for a person to squeeze through.

Without those bubbles, I would never have known it was there. Perfect camouflage.

Excitement fluttered through me and I had to focus on keeping my breathing steady. The map hadn't lied. The cave did exist, hidden beneath years of growth. Tiny bubbles drifted out from the crack, trailing upward like glittering beads on a necklace. My torchlight flickered over them, and I could have sworn they pulsed in rhythm, though that had to be my imagination. Just a trick of the light.

I hovered, weighing the risk. My diving trainer's voice in my head reminded me that unknown caves were dangerous: disorientation, entanglement, equipment damage. But the thrill of discovery drowned out the caution. I'd been diving these waters for years; I knew how to keep my cool. And I simply had to know what was hiding in the darkness. This was my territory, and it almost felt like an affront to find a cave that had been hiding from me.

Taking a deep breath through the regulator, I unclipped my reel and tied the guideline to a jagged spur outside the entrance. It was one of the most important tools a diver carried - the cord would become a lifeline leading me back out if visibility dropped to zero.

One slow fin-kick at a time, I edged forward. The slit widened just enough for me to slip inside, the light from the open sea shrinking to a silver shimmer behind me. The walls were rough and almost black, clearly volcanic in origin. Maybe this was a lava tube. The passage curved downward, and the bubbles grew stronger, fizzing past my mask as though urging me deeper.

I kicked on, heart thudding, into the cave that shouldn't exist. My torchlight cut only a few metres ahead before it was swallowed. I kept one hand on the guideline and forced myself to keep my breathing steady. Slow in, slow out. Don't waste air.

The bubbles thickened the further I went. They streamed from tiny cracks in the stone, glinting in my torchlight like scattered coins. I wondered what was producing them. Volcanic gas? A fissure leading into an air pocket? Whatever it was, the flow never wavered. Almost rhythmic. Almost deliberate.

The passage opened suddenly into a chamber large enough that my beam barely reached the opposite wall. The ceiling arched high above, jagged with rock teeth and draped in algae that swayed as though stirred by some invisible current. Eerily beautiful - but the kind of beauty that whispered *you don't belong here.*

*Get out while you still can.*

When had someone last set eyes on this chamber? The people who'd written about the cave, decades ago, had they ever made it inside? The records didn't mention the bubbles or the rough volcanic walls. Maybe other divers had simply looked at it from the outside and decided not to proceed. Or their equipment had been insufficient, their air cylinders not big enough for such a long dive. Either way, I felt like a true explorer. Even if others had been here before, I was one of a tiny group of people who'd ever seen this cave. It was a momentous thought that almost took my breath away.

I finned further in, checked my pressure gauge. Just over half a tank. Enough time, but not forever. I should turn back soon. Better safe than sorry. Next time, I'd know exactly where the cave was and didn't have to waste time on trying to find it. I'd mark the outside with something to make it easier to retrace my steps. Well, my fin strokes.

That was when the current shifted.

A low groan shuddered through the stone, subtle at first, then deep enough to rattle my ribs. It wasn't the sound of fish or current. It was the sound of weight shifting – of the ocean pressing against a weakness in the cliff. The cave itself seemed to take a breath. A shower of silt rained down, clouding my beam. For a second, I was reminded of a snow globe that someone had just shaken violently.

The ceiling shifted again. Rock teeth ground against each other with a sickening scrape, like bones breaking. Before I could kick back, a slab tore free and tumbled. It hit the floor in a muted crash that echoed in my chest as much as my ears.

I twisted, nearly snagging my hose on a jag of stone. My fins clipped the wall, jolting me sideways. The impact knocked bubbles from my regulator in a frantic rush.

The guideline snapped taut, my tether to the outside quivering in my grip. For one glorious moment, I was relieved - until the cord jerked once, then sagged slack.

My heart plummeted. I tugged at it frantically. No give. It was pinned beneath rubble, my lifeline as trapped as I was.

The water was turning into mud, all visibility swallowed by debris. My pulse hammered in my ears louder than the hiss of the regulator.

The entrance was gone. The only way out... blocked.

Maybe there was a storm raging above the surface. Maybe I should have listened to the alien. Or maybe this had just been a freak accident that could never have been predicted.

Either way, large rocks were in between me and the outside world.

My chest tightened. Not from lack of air, not yet, but from the cold realisation that I was trapped.

4

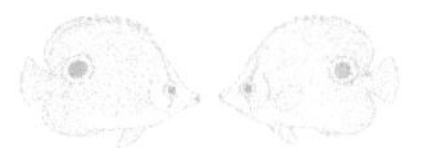

Cerban

The storm was gathering. I could feel it through the soles of my feet as I left the meeting, a deep rumble that made my gills twitch open and closed. It was drawing closer fast. This was going to be a big one.

Outside, the air was heavy with the scent of the oncoming storm, overlaying the salty taste of the sea. Clouds smothered the sun, turning the sky to pewter. Palm fronds snapped in the wind and sand pelted against my legs like tiny stings.

The storm had gained strength faster than I had expected. Humans were running around, dismantling the beach pavilions and removing cushions from recliners. They hadn't expected the weather to change. Maybe I should have warned them. Their technology clearly wasn't good enough at predicting what was about to happen.

I loved a good storm. Swimming deep beneath the surface, feeling the way nature's forces were fighting each other, was one of the best experiences in the world. Surfing the waves while lightning bolts crashed around me, spray hitting my face, the raw power of the wind all-encompassing... Normally, I would have relished the chance to test my strength against nature itself. But today was different.

I was worried.

Was she still out there or had she returned? I had to find out.

I first headed to the small wooden building where she stored her diving equipment. Earlier, when I'd purposely bumped into her, I'd been full of curiosity and excitement. Now, I approached the shack with a very different feeling. What if she was going to get caught by the storm, swept away from the island, lost at sea?

The building was empty. But there was still hope. She didn't live here. Maybe she had returned to her accommodation or one of the common areas reserved for the island's staff. I hurried to the other side of the resort, where humans were running around, preparing for the storm. I wasn't supposed to talk to females, so I approached the closest male. I had never met him before, but I didn't bother with introductions. Time was of the essence.

"Have you seen Maelis?" I asked.

He looked at me suspiciously from beneath a mop of blond hair. "Maelis? The diving instructor? What do you want with her?"

I was tempted to make up an excuse, lie to the male. Instead, I stuck to the truth, hoping that he wouldn't report me to his superiors.

"She mentioned to me earlier that she was going for a dive. I'm worried that she might get caught in the storm. But maybe she didn't go into the water after all. Do you know where she is?"

The male frowned. "I haven't seen her since breakfast. I will ask around. You let me handle this."

I inclined my head in the human fashion. "Thank you. I appreciate it."

This hadn't done anything to calm my fears. If anything, I was even more worried.

She was out there. I was sure of it. She'd gone for a dive and hadn't returned.

I started down the path to the beach, slow at first, forcing myself to breathe evenly. Every step warred with sense. Pam had made the rules clear. *No human staff*. We could not afford another scandal. But my body moved despite orders, despite reason.

In my head, the song she'd been listened to played at full volume. Rise up.

By the time I reached the dunes, the storm had arrived in earnest. Waves rolled against the beach, higher with each set. The spray tasted of copper and earth, stirred from deep places.

I waded in up to my waist, relishing the cold water against my greenskin. The sea spoke in many tongues: the sharp hiss of sand dragged across rock, the hollow boom of waves breaking against the cliffs in the distance, the low, bone-deep growl of stone shifting beneath pressure. The last sound made me freeze in concentration.

Something was wrong deep beneath the waves.

I dived.

The first plunge scoured the world to silence. Beneath the chaos of the surface, the currents were worse - twisting, unpredictable, more violent than they should have been at this depth. Sand and small fish alike swirled in the waves. I kicked hard, cutting through them, following the disturbance where silt streamed up in cloudy banners. My greenskin steadied me while sending information about the currents straight to my brain.

I wasn't used to Earth's oceans. The water tasted less salty, behaved differently. I wasn't sure if I could trust my senses. I had been swimming in this sea many times, but never during a storm.

I angled my body, cutting through the currents in long, strong strokes, letting the water tell me its secrets. Inside, I was begging it to divulge Maelis' location. Nature could be an ally as well as an enemy.

At first, there was nothing. Just scores of reef fish scattering from my approach, shadows vanishing into corals. I scanned the sea with all my senses, trying to pick up the movement of someone larger than these fish. Nothing. There was no trace of her. My chest tightened. Had I been wrong?

Maybe she'd swum further away. The island was the tip of a large column of rock that reached deep into the darkness. I had explored some of it already, including two small caves that cut into the rock. If only I knew where she'd been headed. Down to the caves? Along the reef? Towards one of the other islands? And how far could a human dive anyway? They didn't have gills; they relied on air cylinders. I should have asked Maelis just how much time her cylinder would give her.

I circled wider, skimming along the coral reef until I got to where sand turned to cliff, palms brushing the volcanic rock. Silt hung in the water like storm clouds, stirred by the strengthening current. It coated my skin, clinging in gritty trails.

I dived lower, far into the gloom, and tasted the current with my gills. A metal tang. Air bubbles. Lots of them. I opened my mouth and waited for one of them to pop against my tongue. A faint taste, hard to identify, but I was sure this bubble had not been produced by a living being. This was something else. And it was as good a lead as any to follow.

I increased my pace, my webbed feet beating hard against the churning water. I used the cliff as my guide, descending vertically into the depths.

My greenskin picked up another movement in the rock, a low vibration that made my heart beat faster. The current was pushing against a weakness in the cliff. I had a bad feeling about this.

I found a crevasse and pushed inside, only to discover it narrowed to nothing. My shoulders scraped stone, algae rasping across my arms. Dead end. I reversed out, frustration making my greenskin lash against the water.

Another surge rolled through, carrying with it another thin string of bubbles. They spiralled upward, tingling when they hit my greenskin. Something bugged me about those bubbles. There were too many of them. I turned, following them against the current.

And then, finally, the faint outline of a cave mouth emerged, half-choked with rubble. Algae streamed from its edges like torn banners. Around one jagged rock, a rope had been knotted, its length disappearing beneath a large boulder blocking the entrance. I pressed close, laying my ear against the cold stone. The vibrations were there, erratic and sharp.

A faint heartbeat.

Hers.

Trapped.

Fuck. This was what I had dreaded. Was she injured? Her heartbeat was fast and erratic. It could be because of an injury – or pure, primal fear.

I pushed my hands against the biggest of the rocks. It didn't budge at all. Not that I had expected it to. I had simply hoped against reality.

"Maelis!" I shouted at the top of my voice. "Can you hear me?"

Silence. Of course, she wouldn't be able to respond while using her breathing apparatus. But did I imagine it or did her heart beat even faster?

**Thump**.

Rock hitting rock.

**Thump. Thump.**

Then silence. It had to be her. A signal.

"I will get you out of there!" I yelled.

Three more thumps. She was alive and she was conscious. I had to focus on that. I would deal with everything else once I'd broken through the blockage.

I was tempted to call for my brother and other finmen to help, but that would mean swimming back to the island. I couldn't waste time on that, not when I didn't know how much air Maelis had left. No, I was on my own.

"Can you see another exit? One knock for yes, three for no!"

For a moment, silence. I dreaded the answer. Then, thump, thump, thump. No other exit. That meant I had no other choice but to remove the rocks if I wanted to save her.

It seemed liked an impossible task. The cave mouth was completely blocked. I would need a lever to move some of the boulders, and even that was unlikely to succeed.

I could feel the storm raging far above us as I pulled rock after rock from the rubble, letting them drop into the abyss. I worked as fast as I could, but even that didn't seem fast enough. Occasionally, I would shout, asking whether she could still hear me. Maybe I was imagining it, but I felt like her thumps were getting weaker.

How long would her oxygen last?

5

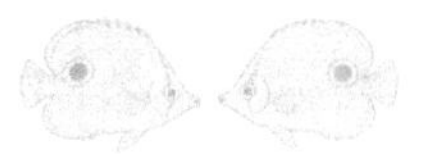

Maelis

The silt hung so thick around me it felt like swimming inside a dust storm. My torch barely cut through the haze; the beam bounced back at me, scattering into useless white glare.

I forced myself to close my eyes and count. *One... two... three...* Slow breaths, steady breaths. My regulator hissed in, hissed out. Each bubble tickled my face before racing upward, desperate to reach the surface I couldn't get to.

The pressure gauge on my cylinder mocked me. The needle had slid deep into the red. Not empty yet, but close. I did the maths automatically – depth, stress consumption, tank size. Ten minutes if I stayed calm. Half that if I didn't.

The wall where the entrance had been loomed like a tombstone. My lifeline – the guideline – vanished beneath a slab of rock as though it had never existed. I tugged once more out of sheer desperation, but it stayed buried. My pulse thudded harder, too fast, stealing air I couldn't spare.

I clenched my fists. *Stop. Think.* That was what every instructor drilled into us. Panicked divers died. Calm divers sometimes lived.

But calm was a joke in a sealed cave with only a handful of breaths left.

The vibrations reached me then. A faint tremor in the rock that brushed against my mask. I froze, straining to listen. Not stone this time. Not collapse. A voice, faint but unmistakable, distorted by water.

A man. He was able to talk underwater, which could only mean one thing: he was a finman. The voice sounded familiar, but I couldn't be sure.

I banged the nearest rock with my fist, three sharp thuds. My knuckles stung, but the sound carried. Again, three thuds. Then I clutched the regulator in both hands, as if holding it tighter would coax more air from it.

The silt shifted as he pulled at the rubble outside. I couldn't see him, but I felt his presence through the water, the stubborn persistence of someone who refused to let go. For a heartbeat, hope flared bright enough to make me dizzy.

Then the regulator sputtered. Just once, a hiccup in the steady hiss.

My blood turned to ice. The tank was almost done.

Dark spots drifted at the edges of my vision, and it took all my strength not to rip the mask from my face in panic. I pressed my fist against the rock one more time – weak now, barely more than a tap.

I was out of time.

The regulator wheezed again, a hollow rattle that sent dread clawing up my spine. My lungs screamed for more, but I forced them to take tiny sips, stretching the last dribbles of air.

Then – light.

A thin beam lanced through the rubble, slicing into the murk. Rock scraped against rock outside, followed by a sudden rush of bubbles as a stone shifted free. Water swirled into the gap, pulling silt away, widening just enough to reveal a wedge of green skin.

His face pressed through the crack, algae filaments streaming behind him like ribbons. For a moment I thought I was hallucinating, but then his eyes locked on mine – sharp, steady, anchoring me.

It was him. I had hoped it... but here he was, the alien whose name I didn't even know. The finman who'd predicted the storm I hadn't foreseen. He smiled at me, but his expression was tense.

"I will get you out of there."

His lips moved before the words reached my ears. It all felt very surreal. Maybe I was hallucinating him. I wouldn't be surprised, given my desperate state.

"How much air do you have left?" he asked, his gaze intense.

I couldn't talk, unlike him, so I just shook my head dejectedly. He got the message. His eyes widened. He looked at the regulator, then peered into the dark cave behind me. Maybe his vision was better than mine, but even with the torchlight, I hadn't seen another exit. The tunnel quickly became too narrow for me to swim. I was trapped. I didn't need the alien to tell me that.

The regulator hissed a last thin stream, then fell silent. My lungs convulsed, desperate, dragging only seawater against the seal of my mask. Black specks swarmed the edges of my vision. I reached out, grasping for something, anything-

He grasped my hand in a strong grip that I would never have been able to escape from and pulled me towards the hole. I wouldn't fit through it. No way. Neither would he. It was pointless.

My lungs burned with a fierce pain. Then his face was there, centre of my diminishing vision. His eyes bored into me, steady, commanding: *trust me.*

He tore the regulator from my mouth. I tried to fight him, thrashing with panic, but he caught my jaw in one firm hand. And then his mouth sealed over mine.

Air surged into me. Not from the failing tank, but warm and rich, fed from his own lungs. My chest expanded, my vision cleared. A sob of relief slipped into the bubbles between us.

When he drew back, his gills flared wide, fanning the water. He inhaled deep, filtering the sea as though it were nothing, then bent to me again. Another rush of life, another kiss that left me shaking.

I clutched his arm, nails digging into slick green skin, terrified he might stop. But he didn't. Again and again, he gave me breath, each exchange binding me closer to him, even as the rocks held me fast.

Alive, but not free. Not yet.

We couldn't stay like this forever. He'd managed to squeeze his head and one arm through the hole, but that meant he was now just as trapped as I was. If he wanted to continue clearing the rubble, he'd have to stop breathing for me.

The world had narrowed to a rhythm: darkness pressing in, the crush of rock around me, and then his mouth sealing over mine to deliver another precious rush of air. Each time, my lungs burned a little less, my panic ebbed a little more. Each time, I realised just how close we were, how much of my survival now depended on him.

I should have been terrified of the alien pressed against me, of his sharp teeth and the strange tendrils that drifted from his skin. Instead, I was terrified of him leaving.

The cave groaned again, a vibration that rattled my bones. Pebbles sifted down from the ceiling, bouncing off my mask. I flinched, my chest tightening all over again. My hand closed around his wrist, hard, begging him not to go, not to leave me alone in the dark.

His eyes caught mine through the haze of silt, glowing faintly with their own light. He shook his head, firm, steady, and pressed his mouth to mine again. Another gift of air, another reprieve.

The regulator floated uselessly at my shoulder now, hose limp. My tank was dead weight. I wanted to strip it off, to squeeze through the gap, to fight free – but the rubble held me too tight. I couldn't move without the rock biting into my ribs and hips.

Helpless. If I thought about it too much, the panic would rise again. Instead, I fixed my gaze on him. The finman. My unlikely lifeline. He shifted his shoulders against the crack, testing the stones, and I felt the pressure change as he tried to widen the gap. Every scrape echoed through the water, but the boulders refused to yield.

This was pointless. We were trapped in a moment, a continuous rhythm that couldn't go on for much longer. At some point, he would realise that he couldn't both give me the air I needed and free me at the same time. We couldn't stay like this forever. Would he give up on me?

I was human. I wasn't the same species as him. If he was anything like Kelon, his former leader, he'd run.

His lips met mine again and I sucked in the offered air greedily.

Then I noticed it. The bubbles. The same ones that had lured me down here in the first place. Some weren't vanishing into the water – they were gathering above, trapped against the jagged ceiling of the cave.

An air pocket.

I jabbed my finger upward, desperate for him to understand. He frowned, then followed my gaze. His eyes widened in understanding. Then he nodded. He gave me another kiss of air.

With the last of my strength, I kicked upward, wriggling past the rubble until my head broke the surface.

Air. Stale, sour, tinged with minerals. But I wasn't going to complain. I could breathe.

This bubble wouldn't last long, but it was enough to keep me breathing for a moment. Hopefully, it would be enough time for him to create a larger hole.

"Do you have enough oxygen up there?" he called through the water. His voice sounded like it was coming through a long tunnel.

"Yes." I was amazed I could speak. "I think so."

In truth, I didn't know the oxygen concentration of this air bubble. But my lungs weren't straining, which was a good sign. I hoped.

I turned, heart pounding, to the shadow in the crack. He'd wedged his head and shoulders through, gills flaring in the gloom.

He smiled at me. "You are safe. For now."

My laugh came out broken. "Not exactly the pep talk I wanted."

He tilted his head, teeth flashing. "Then tell me what you need to hear, human."

"My name's Maelis," I said hoarsely. "And I'm not giving up. Tell me you're not giving up on me. Tell me you won't leave me down here."

Something flared in his eyes. "Never."

I believed him.

And for the first time since the collapse, I believed that I might yet return to the surface. Alive.

6

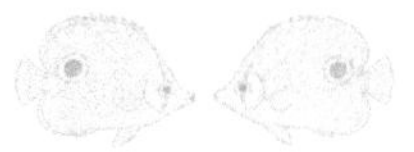

Cerban

Every muscle in my body burned as I wrenched at the rocks blocking the cave mouth. The sea fought me with every surge of the storm, trying to drive me back, but I refused. I was not leaving her behind.

Piece by piece, I shifted the smaller stones, letting them tumble into the abyss. Each time I moved one, more silt bled into the water, blinding me. My gills stung from the grit, my shoulders scraped raw where the jagged rock tore at them. Still, I pushed on.

Inside, I caught the faint sound of her fists striking the stone in rhythm with me. She was helping – weak, but stubborn. The thought filled me with a savage pride. This human was no helpless prey. She was fighting for her life, and I would match her strike for strike.

At last, the biggest boulder shifted. I jammed my shoulder against it, wedging my body in the gap. My spine screamed, but slowly, agonisingly, the stone moved. The opening widened enough for her small frame to squeeze through.

"Do you think you'll fit through this?" I called out.

"I believe so. I can't believe you actually did it. I thought I'd be trapped here forever - well, until my air ran out."

I shuddered at the thought. Finfolk couldn't drown, but I imagined it as a horrible death.

"When I say so, swim to me and hold on tight. I'll get us back to the surface. Any time you need a break or have to breathe, squeeze my shoulder. I'll go as fast or slow as you need."

I heard her take a deep breath before she replied, her voice shaking despite her determined tone. "Yes. I'm ready."

I breathed in a few times as deep as I could, filling my lungs with oxygen. I could hold my breath for a few minutes if needed, giving me the chance to share my air with her without having to stop swimming. Soon, we'd be back on land. If the Tidebound was here, I'd take her to the medbay to get scanned from top to bottom, making sure that she hadn't sustained injuries during her misadventure. But the spaceship was far away. We'd have to rely on human technology. I didn't know if there was a medic on the island. If not, I'd... I'd figure it out when we got there.

First, I had to bring her back to the surface.

I gritted my teeth and steadied myself. "I need you to swim through the gap now. Don't be afraid. We shall get through this."

Together, I wanted to add. But I didn't want her to think I was doing this for any other reason than to save her life.

"Alright, I'm coming!"

She took one last deep breath, then she swam to the entrance. I tasted blood in the water. She was bleeding from several scratches on her arms and hands. How had I not noticed that before? I must have been too focused on getting rid of the rubble.

And then she was in my arms, body trembling. She was so small. So vulnerable. I grasped her head, forced her to look at me. There was fear in her eyes, but there was also hope. I clung to that. I would be her hope. I would save her.

I pressed my lips to hers, trying hard to ignore how good it felt. This was just to give her the air she needed. It was not a kiss. Nothing like that. She sucked in my breath, then leaned back, breaking the not-a-kiss.

As I turned us, something caught my eye: bubbles still streaming from cracks in the cave wall. Not the random scatter of air, but pulsing, steady, almost purposeful. My gills flared, tasting their metallic tang. Strange. Important, maybe. But not now.

She was my priority. And deep inside I knew that she'd always be that. Even if she didn't know it yet.

I powered upwards, cutting through the storm-churned sea. Waves battered me, lightning flashed faintly through the water, but I didn't stop. Every few strokes, I'd breathe for her. She was clinging to me still, but her grip was growing weaker. Despite that, I stayed beneath the surface even when we had ascended all the way. It would be faster to swim back to the island underneath the wild waves.

I drew on my last reserves of energy to propel us through the angry sea. As we got closer and closer to the island, the coral reef appeared beneath us, strangely peaceful despite everything that had happened. Many of the colourful fish had sought shelter amongst the coral and rocks, but a few were swimming happily despite the pull of the currents.

When at last we broke the surface, it was chaos. Waves rose higher than my shoulders, slamming against us with the force of battering rams. Rain lashed down, stinging my eyes, while the wind howled so loud it swallowed her gasps.

She clung to me weakly, too spent to fight the sea on her own. I wrapped one arm around her chest, keeping her head above the waves, and struck out with the other. My legs drove against the current, every kick a battle.

Lightning flared, turning the water silver for a heartbeat. It showed me the breakers ahead – white foam hammering the shallows of the beach. Getting through them would be dangerous. But the shore was close. Not much longer and she'd be safe from the brutal forces of nature.

"Hold on!" I shouted, though I doubted she heard me. Her hands clawed at my arm anyway, and that was answer enough.

The first breaker hit, tumbling us beneath a mountain of foam. I tucked her against me, twisting so my back took the brunt of the surge. The pressure crushed us down, then spat us out, tumbling end over end. We surfaced coughing, but alive. Another breaker loomed.

I timed it – one deep breath, one powerful surge of my legs – and we rode the crest. It hurled us forward, slamming my knees into sand. My greenskin flared with pain. I staggered upright, half-carrying, half-dragging her through the sucking pull of the retreating wave.

At last, the sea let us go. I carried her up the beach, away from the grasp of the foam, until the dunes broke the worst of the wind. There I set her down gently on the wet sand.

She was trembling violently, lips blue, eyes dazed. I brushed the tangled hair from her face, listening. Her breaths came in ragged bursts. Too fast. Too shallow.

"Breathe," I urged softly, crouching close so my words cut through the roar of the storm. "Slow. In. Out."

She tried. Failed. Coughed seawater. I tilted her onto her side until she spat it out, then steadied her again. Relief shuddered through me when her chest rose more evenly.

I laid my hand against her sternum, feeling the frantic flutter of her heart. Was this a normal rhythm for a human? It felt too quick for my liking. But it was strong. She was alive.

"You will not die," I told her fiercely. Whether she understood or not, I didn't care. The words were a promise, as binding as any oath.

The storm raged above us, but for that moment all I could hear was her fragile breathing – and the vow echoing in my blood that I would keep it going.

Her breathing steadied little by little, but the colour of her lips still frightened me. She was too pale, her skin clammy beneath my hand. Humans were fragile. Too fragile. I had no way of knowing if water had reached her lungs, if she would worsen once the shock passed.

On Finfolkaheem, healers would already be swarming her, pressing hot poultices to her chest, forcing her to rest until her strength returned. Here, I had nothing. No Tidebound. No finfolk medic.

I'd have to take her to the humans. They'd know what to do.

But to seek help meant confessing. Pam had warned us clearly: no contact with the staff. No exceptions. After Kelon's disgrace, every rule had been sharpened to a blade. If I carried Maelis to a human medic, there would be questions I could not answer without exposing us both.

I looked down at her again. Her lashes trembled against her cheeks, her chest rising too shallowly. She needed a healer. Not rules. Not politics. A healer.

"I should not have spoken to you," I murmured. "I should have turned away when I saw you dance." The words tore at my throat. "But if the price for saving you is punishment, then so be it."

She stirred faintly, her lips parting as if she wanted to speak, but no sound came. My heart clenched. I bent closer and gathered her into my arms. She felt far too light, limp as seagrass, head lolling against my shoulder. I adjusted my grip, so her face was turned away from the rain and started up the beach.

The wind clawed at me, dragging at her damp hair, driving salt into my eyes, but I didn't slow. Each step sank into wet sand, but still I pushed on, muscles aching from the dive and the fight against the current.

The resort's lights glimmered faintly through the sheets of rain, my only beacon. Somewhere in those buildings were humans trained in medicine. They would know how to ease her breathing, how to prevent hidden injuries from stealing her away later.

Pam would rage. Paul would lecture. Rainse might even laugh at my stupidity. None of it mattered.

Rules could be mended. Reputations rebuilt. A life could not.

I tightened my hold on Maelis and strode faster toward the cluster of lights, my gills burning with every breath of storm air. Whatever punishment awaited me, I would face it. But first... She had to live.

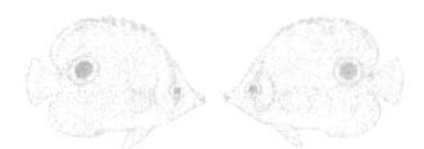

## 7

Maelis

The first thing I noticed when I woke was a steady hum and the feeling of cool air on my face. A mask was strapped over my face, offering sweet, refreshing oxygen.

The second was the argument.

"She needs rest," Paul was saying, his voice tight with authority. "And you need to go. You've done enough already."

"No," came the reply, low and rough as the sea at night. The alien. The finman. I still didn't know his name. "I will not leave her."

I blinked against the dim light until the room swam into focus. The infirmary was no bigger than a broom closet with a bed shoved in, cupboards along one wall, and a humming oxygen cylinder at my side. Rain rattled the small window, proof that the storm hadn't yet blown itself out.

I'd only been in here a few times, mostly to accompany resort visitors who'd got sunburnt or who'd got in touch with jellyfish. The only time I'd ever needed medical care myself had been a large scrape on my arm sustained while diving - I'd misjudged the distance between me and a coral.

But I did know the nurse, Tyrone, very well. He was a shy guy who rarely joined the staff parties, but I'd had many friendly conversations with him. When it was just the two of us, he came out of his shell. Now, he was fussing with a clipboard but throwing anxious looks at the two men squared off beside me. Paul, damp and red-faced, blocking the door as though he could bar a wall of muscle with his sheer disapproval. The finman stood tall and immovable, seawater still dripping from the algae clinging to his shoulders.

My saviour.

The memory came back in jolts: the cave collapsing, the blackness closing in, his mouth sealing over mine, warm air flooding my lungs. The terror, the trust. His arms carrying me through the storm as if I weighed nothing at all. I dimly remembered lying on sand, but then it all went blank. He must have brought me here.

"I told you, she'll be monitored here until the weather clears," Tyrone said briskly. I was proud of him for standing his ground. "Once it's safe, she'll need to be flown out to a hospital. Hyperbaric chamber, just in case. But right now, rest and warmth are all that matter until the storm clears and the airport reopens."

"I can watch her," the finman growled. "If her heart changes, I will hear it. If her breathing falters, I will know."

Paul pinched the bridge of his nose. "That's not how this works. We can't have staff and... guests... mixing. You know the rules."

I shifted weakly, my hand tugging at the blanket. The movement silenced them both. Two sets of eyes – one human, one alien – snapped to me.

"Maelis," Paul said quickly, relief in his tone. "Don't try to talk. You're safe. You–"

"I'm fine," I croaked, pushing the mask off my face. "It was just a bit of seawater."

Tyrone glared at me. "Your blood oxygen levels are way lower than they should be. And if what Cerban here is saying is true, you resurfaced too fast. You could end up with decompression sickness. If I had my way, you'd be on a plane to the nearest hospital. But as all planes and helicopters are grounded until the storm lessens, you will stay here, under my constant observation."

The bends. Not good. Down in the cave, all I'd wanted had been to be back on the island. I'd forgotten to tell the alien that he should resurface slowly, taking breaks at regular intervals. He wouldn't have known that human bodies weren't made for being underwater.

I almost laughed. Every time I took clients for a dive, I explained to them the risks of decompression sickness. I should have known better. At the same time, I would be dead if it hadn't been for him. Wait, Tyrone had said his name.

*Cerban.*

I tasted it on my tongue. It felt perfect.

"Are you warm enough?" Tyrone asked, more gently this time.

"I could do with another blanket, if you have one."

He tsked. "I have plenty of blankets. I even have an electric blanket stashed away somewhere. Don't think I've ever actually used it, but there is a first time for everything."

While Tyrone spread a bright orange blanket over me, Paul rolled his shoulder as if preparing for a fight.

"You've done enough," the resort manager said again, his voice like steel. "You're not staying here. Not in this room. Not with her."

Cerban's gills flared as if he was drawing in seawater, his entire frame vibrating with contained fury. "She lives because of me. You would have let her drown!"

"I didn't even know she was out for a dive! And that's not the point!" Paul snapped, stepping closer, jaw set. "There are rules for a reason. You broke them, and you'll answer for it. Right now, the priority is her recovery, not your pride. Once she is better, we will discuss what happened in detail."

I wanted to tell them both to shut up. My head throbbed with every raised word, and all I wanted was quiet, warmth, and a large sip of water to get the taste of salt out of my mouth. But I couldn't look away from the finman – Cerban. His name still rolled through my mind, strong and dependable as the tide.

He leaned closer, his eyes on me, not Paul. "I will not leave you." The words weren't a promise, they were a vow; deep and unyielding.

"Like hell you won't," Paul barked. "This isn't negotiable." He nodded to Tyrone. "Back me up."

The nurse hesitated, shifting from foot to foot, then gave a reluctant sigh. "Cerban, she's stable for now. If you want what's best for her, you'll let me monitor her without... distractions. I'll call you if anything changes."

The finman's jaw flexed, sharp teeth flashing as he ground them together. For a heartbeat I thought he'd fight, that he'd toss Paul aside and plant himself like a sentry at my bedside. Then his eyes returned to mine, searching, asking.

I didn't have the strength for words, but I managed the smallest nod, whispering past cracked lips. "I'll be all right."

His shoulders slumped, defeat pressed into every line of his body.

"I will return," he rumbled. A promise I knew he'd keep.

Only then did he back away, every movement reluctant, until Paul shoved the door open and gestured him out. The finman cast one last look at me over his shoulder, a gaze heavy with meaning, before vanishing into the corridor.

The room felt colder without him, even under two blankets.

"I will have a chat with Pam and Fionn," Paul said, turning to the door. "I will be back soon. Let me know if you need anything. And Maelis... I'm glad you're alright."

When the door clicked shut behind him, I sagged into the pillows, exhausted by the tension that had sizzled between the two men.

Tyrone busied himself at the small sink, filling a cup before carrying it over. "Here," he said gently, sliding a hand behind my shoulders to help me sit. "Small sips. Your lungs don't need any more surprises tonight."

The water was cool and clean, a far cry from the salt and grit I'd coughed up on the beach. It soothed my raw throat, though my voice still rasped when I asked, "He... carried me out?"

Tyrone gave a short, almost nervous laugh. "Carried you, fought the surf with you in his arms, then stormed straight in here demanding I treat you before I could even check his own injuries. I'd say you've made quite an impression."

Heat prickled my cheeks. "I didn't exactly ask him to."

"No," Tyrone agreed, setting the cup aside. "But you'd be dead without him. You know that, right? I've seen near-drownings. Most don't walk away. You will, thanks to him."

I swallowed hard. "Cerban," I murmured, tasting the name again.

Tyrone arched a brow. "He told you his name?"

"I overheard you."

"Ah." He scratched the back of his neck, glancing toward the door. "He's... different from the others. Quieter. Keeps to himself most of the time, but when he does speak up, everyone listens. Pam says he's steady as bedrock. Some of the staff think he's brooding. Me?"

Tyrone shrugged. "I think he's dangerous – but only if you're a threat to someone he cares about."

Dangerous. The word should have made me recoil. Instead, it curled warm in my chest.

I sank back into the pillows, the oxygen mask hissing softly beside me. "He wouldn't leave."

"No," Tyrone said, a wry smile tugging at his mouth. "I don't think he's the sort who leaves, not if he's decided you matter."

That thought followed me into the quiet that fell between us, the storm outside rattling the windows, the weight of his vow still echoing in my ears.

Not long ago, Cerban had been everything that stood between me and certain death. Down in the depths of the ocean, rules hadn't mattered. I hadn't cared that he was an alien and I was human. For a while, I'd forgotten that I disliked aliens. Now we were back on the surface, back in reality. Even if I dropped all my previous reservations, it was against the island's rules for the two of us to spend time together.

So was I supposed to just forget what he'd done for me and continue as before? I didn't think I could do that.

He'd saved my life. I was in his debt. And I was sure as hell going to repay that debt.

Even if it went against the rules.

8

Cerban

Rainse waited for me outside. News had travelled fast. He took one look at me, then clasped me in a tight embrace.

"Brother. How is she?"

"Weak, but she will live. They might have to transport her to a different island if her condition worsens."

He let out a long breath, the tension in his shoulders easing a fraction. "Then you did what needed to be done."

"Yes." My jaw tightened. "But the humans will not see it that way."

He gave me a crooked smile, the kind he reserved for

when he thought rules were meant to be broken. "Pam already knows?"

"She will," I said grimly. "Paul saw everything. He was in the room when I refused to leave."

Rainse's expression sobered. "Then you'll have to answer for it. She won't forgive another breach so soon after Kelon's disgrace."

The mention of our former captain soured the water in my veins. Kelon's crime had stained all of us, and now my actions would only deepen the mistrust. But the thought of leaving Maelis trapped in that cave, of ignoring her heartbeat pounding against the stone... impossible.

"Would you have acted any differently?" I asked my clutch-brother.

He thought for a moment. "I don't think so, no. Maybe I would have tried to stop her from going into the water in the first place, but it was hard to predict just how hard the storm would hit the island. And she is an adult. She bears responsibility for her own actions. But I don't have all the information. All I've been told is that you made yourself suspicious by asking about the diving instructor before appearing with her hours later, both of you in bad shape. Are you alright? Are you injured?"

"I am fine. A few scrapes, nothing to worry about. And I could sleep for an entire sunpass."

"I doubt Paul and Pam will let you sleep that long." He chuckled.

And he was right. We hadn't even reached the accommodations when one of the finmen intercepted us, breathless. "You're wanted in the comms room. Now."

The words churned my stomach. Of course.

Rainse came with me, and together we entered the small, brightly lit chamber in the heart of the building assigned to the finfolk. A holo-screen dominated the far wall. Paul stood stiffly to one side, arms crossed. The connection was already active. Pam's face filled the projection, every line sharpened by her fury. Fionn and Elise hovered in the background, silent but watching. I wasn't sure if it was lucky or unlucky for them to be with Pam right in this moment. My clutch-brother gave me a small nod, barely noticeable. I knew he'd be on my side, and that was a relief beyond bounds. The humans respected him as the first finman to find a human mate.

"There you are," Pam said, her voice clipped. "Explain yourself."

I squared my shoulders, ready for the fight that was sure to come. "A human was drowning. I saved her."

"That is not the issue," Paul snapped, but Pam silenced him with a raised hand.

"The rules exist for a reason, Cerban. After Kelon, every mistake is magnified. And now I hear you defied Paul, carried a staff member into the resort in front of witnesses, and refused to leave her bedside. Do you understand what this looks like?"

"I understand she would be dead if I had obeyed your rules," I said, each word heavy as stone.

Pam's lips thinned. She opened her mouth, but Fionn spoke first, his voice calm but carrying the weight of command.

"Pam. Paul." His gaze cut to each of them in turn before landing on me. "Cerban is my brother. I know his heart. He does not act rashly. If he chose to intervene, it is because there was no other choice."

Pam's brow furrowed. "That doesn't excuse–"

"It does not excuse," Fionn interrupted gently, respectful but firm. "But it explains. And it shows that he put the life of a human above his own safety and above our reputation. That is what we promised when we came here. To be better than Kelon. To earn trust."

Paul shifted uncomfortably but didn't speak. Elise leaned forward into the projection. "I was there when Kelon almost ruined everything. If Cerban had left Maelis to drown, what would that have proven? That we care more about rules than lives? That would have destroyed trust far worse."

Pam exhaled sharply, the sound distorting in the holo-feed. "Be that as it may, rules are not suggestions. Cerban, you are confined to quarters until further notice. No contact with staff. If you break that order, you will be recalled to Finfolkaheem. Is that clear?"

Technically, she had no authority over me and the finmen - and yet she did. She had close contact with the Intergalactic Authority. They could revoke our licence to be on this planet at any moment. And if Pam decided to remove us from her dating agency... it would affect not just me, but all the other finmen who'd travelled with me on the Tidebound, my clutch-brothers included.

I inclined my head, though inside, the vow I'd made on the beach burned hotter than ever. "Clear."

Fionn's eyes met mine through the projection, steady and strong. He gave the smallest of smiles – silent solidarity, even as he upheld the rules.

Pam ended the call, the holo-screen dissolving into darkness. Paul turned on his heel without a word and left the room.

Rainse muttered a curse under his breath. He leaned against the wall, arms folded, studying me with a mix of amusement and concern.

"That went well."

I wasn't sure if he was joking. I let out a growl, low and sharp. "I would do it again. A hundred times."

He smirked faintly. "I know. That's why I'm standing here instead of dragging you back to your quarters by the greenskin like Pam would prefer." He straightened, stepping closer. "Tell me, though. Why this human? What is she to you?"

I hesitated, the words heavy in my throat. But hiding them was useless. He already knew.

"She is mine," I said.

Rainse's brows rose, but he didn't laugh. He just studied me, sharp-eyed. "You're certain?"

"Yes." The memory of her heartbeat echoed in my chest, calling to mine with a rhythm older than the tides. "When I heard her in that cave, it was not duty that drove me. It was need. As if the sea itself would not let me live if I let her die."

"And your greenskin...?"

"Tense as my cock when I'm close to her."

Rainse laughed. "Smooth as always, brother. But she hasn't shown up as a match for you. You're in the database. It would have come up in the latest results."

"Not if Maelis isn't in the database. She's staff on the island. She is not one of the females sent here to find a mate."

"I guess we can't ask Pam just now to confirm."

I chuckled despite myself. "No, I doubt that would be received well."

"They will want proof. Paul, Pam and the others won't let you anywhere near her unless you can prove that she's your mate."

I clenched my fists, nails biting into my palms. "Rules. Always rules. Yet the rules would have left her dead at the bottom of the sea. What good are they, if they deny what is true?"

Rainse clapped a hand to my shoulder. "Easy. I'm on your side. But if you mean to fight for her, you'd better be ready. Because proving she's your mate when the agency says otherwise..." He shook his head, lips quirking. "That's going to make the storm outside look like a gentle wave."

I met his gaze, steady. "Then let it come. No force in this world or the next will keep me from her."

Rainse's smirk faded into something more serious. He nodded once. "Then we'll face it together. Tell me how I can help."

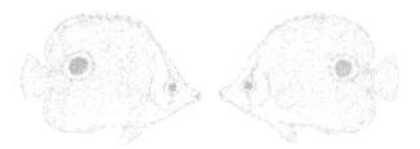

Maelis

By morning, the storm had passed. The sky outside the infirmary window was scrubbed clean, an endless stretch of blue broken only by drifting white clouds. The palm trees still leaned sideways, salt-crusted and battered, but the wind had lost its teeth.

I, however, was still stuck in bed.

Tyrone had fussed over me since dawn, checking my vitals, making me sip water and nibble dry biscuits, reminding me every few minutes that I'd *nearly drowned*. I was grateful, really – but also bored out of my skull. There are only so many ways to count ceiling tiles before you start to lose it.

At least my dive camera had survived. Tyrone had retrieved my gear, setting it on the chair by my bed.

The wetsuit reeked of salt and algae, but the little waterproof housing with my camera inside was mercifully intact. I powered it on, fast-forwarding through the first dull minutes of me swimming along the reef.

When the footage reached the cave, my breath hitched. Seeing it from the safety of the infirmary was surreal. I pulled the blanket closer to myself. The torchlight darted over jagged rock, the silt clouded the view, and then came the collapse – my world turning into a storm of dust and shadow.

But it wasn't the rockfall that made me sit up straighter. It was the bubbles.

On the recording, they rose in streams along the cave wall. Not the erratic fizz of trapped air pockets. No, these were steady, deliberate, pulsing with a rhythm. Five bursts, pause. Five bursts, pause. Over and over again, even as the rocks crumbled.

I scrubbed back and replayed it, leaning so close my forehead almost hit the screen. It wasn't natural. Couldn't be.

A shiver ran down my spine. I'd thought the bubbles were just a trick of the currents in the moment, but now, safe and dry, I could see it clearly: a pattern. Almost like counting.

I sank back into the pillows, clutching the camera to my chest. Whatever those bubbles were, they hadn't been random. And something told me the finman – Cerban – had noticed them too.

I was still staring at the looping footage when the door creaked open and Tyrone slipped inside, balancing a tray with a steaming mug and another round of dry biscuits.

"You're supposed to be resting," he chided gently.

"I am," I said, though the way my heart was racing at the sight on the screen made it a lie. I turned the camera so he could see. "Look. Tell me I'm not imagining this."

He set the tray down and leaned over my shoulder. On the little display, the bubbles rose again in their strange rhythm – five bursts, pause, five bursts, pause.

Tyrone frowned. "That's... odd. Could be gas trapped in the rock, but I've never seen it come out that evenly before."

"So you see it too. I thought maybe I was losing it."

"No, you're not losing it." He straightened, rubbing the back of his neck. "But whatever it is, it's not my field. I patch up jellyfish stings, Maelis, I don't explain geology."

Still, the look in his eyes said he found it just as unsettling as I did.

I sank back against the pillows. "It doesn't feel natural. Like it was... counting."

"Counting?" He gave a small snort, though there wasn't much humour in it. "That's a stretch."

"Maybe," I muttered, but the unease gnawed at me.

Tyrone busied himself with the mug, pressing it into my hands. "Drink. Hot tea fixes most things."

"Do they teach that in nursing school?"

He laughed and busied himself with the monitors tracking my vitals.

I sipped obediently. The warmth helped, though it didn't stop my brain racing.

"There's something else you should know," Tyrone said after a moment. His voice had shifted, quieter now. "Pam was on a call last night. With Paul, and your rescuer. Cerban."

I stilled. "And?"

His expression was troubled. "She wasn't pleased. The finfolk are under strict orders not to interfere with staff. You know that. After what Kelon did... Well. Cerban's actions are being treated as a serious breach."

My stomach dropped. "He saved my life."

"I know. And Pam and Paul both know that as well, but they have to stand firm on this. If they ignore what he did, that will open the door to other finmen going against the rules. For now, Cerban is confined to quarters. He's not allowed to be around humans, not even men. No contact with staff. No exceptions. I don't know if they put a time limit on it, but for now, that's what it is."

Confined. The word sat heavy in my chest.

I closed my eyes, replaying the moment in the cave when his mouth pressed to mine, sharing breath, sharing life. The moment he carried me through the storm as if nothing could tear me from his arms.

"No exceptions," I echoed softly.

Tyrone shifted uncomfortably. "I'm sorry. I know he's the reason you're alive. But the rules are what they are."

Rules. Always rules.

I opened my eyes and stared back at the tiny screen where the bubbles pulsed on an endless loop. Patterns in the dark, waiting to be deciphered.

And somehow, I knew Cerban was the only one who could help me understand them.

I set the mug down with a little more force than necessary. "Tyrone."

He glanced up, wary. "Hmm?"

"Can you get a message to him?"

His eyes widened. "Absolutely not. Pam was very clear–"

"I don't care what Pam said." My voice was hoarse but steady. "I just... I need to thank him. Properly. Not while half-drowning in a cave, not while hooked up to your machine here. I need to look him in the eye and say it."

Tyrone hesitated, lips pressed into a thin line.

"You know me," I pressed. "I'm not reckless." His eyebrow shot up, and I sighed. "Okay, not usually reckless. But this isn't about breaking rules for fun. He risked everything for me. If Pam wants to lecture someone, she can lecture me too."

For a long moment he studied me, and I thought he'd refuse. Then he muttered something under his breath and fiddled with his clipboard. "I'll... see what I can do. No promises."

Relief unfurled in my chest. "Thank you."

He shook his head, muttering again as he gathered the tray. "You're trouble, Maelis. That finman's not the only one who's going to end up in hot water."

As the door clicked shut behind him, I smiled faintly, settling back into the pillows. Trouble or not, I wasn't going to let Cerban's defiance be for nothing.

With Tyrone gone, I went back to watching the camera footage while slowly sipping my tea. The rhythm was so obvious now, it was hard to believe I hadn't spotted it back in the cave. But then, I'd had other concerns then. Like staying alive.

Without the bubbles, I wouldn't have found the cave. And if the cave hadn't collapsed, I would have noticed the pattern.

I tried to relax, tried to sleep, but my thoughts kept returning to the cave. I'd never been that close to death before.

Not really. Scrapes, stings, bruises – those were part of the job. But staring at the last few breaths in my tank, lungs seizing while the rock pressed in on all sides... that had been different.

For a while in that darkness, I'd accepted it. That this was how it ended. That my body would be another secret the sea kept, swallowed whole like so many before me.

The thought left me cold, even beneath Tyrone's triple blanket.

And yet... the bubbles.

If they'd been random, I'd have dismissed them, buried the memory along with the fear. But they weren't. They pulsed with intent. They had led me to the cave, and when the collapse came, they'd revealed the air pocket that bought me precious minutes.

Maybe it was madness, but I couldn't see them as coincidence any more. They'd turned the cave from a tomb into a puzzle. A message.

And puzzles, unlike tombs, could be solved.

The idea steadied me. I wasn't ready to dive again – not yet. The thought of sliding back into that narrow passage made my chest seize. But one day I would. And when I did, I wouldn't just be a diver chasing thrill and beauty. I'd be chasing answers.

That cave had nearly killed me. The bubbles gave me a reason to go back. A way to make the fear mean something. To change a painful memory into something positive.

I drained the last of the tea, set the mug aside, and whispered into the quiet room, "Next time, I'll be ready."

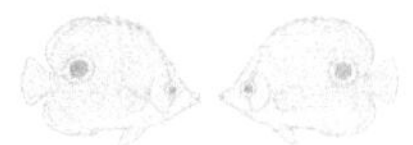

Cerban

I paced back and forth in my room, which suddenly appeared far too small for a grown finman. How long had it been? How many sunpasses had it been since I'd left her with the medic? It felt like an eternity. Rainse had been my only visitor - and without him, I would have long left the finmen's quarters and gone in search of Maelis.

I missed her - and yet I didn't even know her. If I'd been allowed to talk to human staff, I would have interrogated them about her. Because I couldn't, Rainse was on a mission to find out everything he could about Maelis.

Now he lounged on the edge of my bunk, watching me pace like a caged predator. "She's stable. That much I know."

I stopped, gripping the doorframe until my claws scored the wood. "Stable is not enough. She nearly drowned. Humans are fragile. What if her lungs fail? What if she worsens in the night?"

Rainse tilted his head, studying me with that infuriatingly calm look. "You already told me she's your mate. So, act like it. Protect her by not making things worse with Pam and Paul."

My gills flared wide, aching with the stale air of my confinement. "Patience does not keep her safe."

He smirked. "No, but breaking out of quarters will only get you shipped home in chains. You want to keep her? You'll need a smarter plan."

I growled low in my throat, frustration clawing at me. "Smarter plans do not ease the ache of being kept from her side."

Rainse grinned, unbothered by my temper. "Then maybe this will." He pulled a folded scrap of paper from his belt, holding it between two fingers. "From your human. A message."

My heart slammed against my ribs. "Give it."

He handed it over without fuss. "She wanted to thank you. Properly. Not through doctors or rules. Just... thank you."

I clutched the note, her uneven script alive beneath my

fingertips. Every letter was proof: she was thinking of me too.

Rainse leaned back, folding his arms. "So, brother. What's your next move? Sit here and pine? Or find a way to prove to her – and to everyone else – that she's yours?"

I stared at the note, pulse thrumming. There was no choice. There never had been.

> *Cerban,*
> *Thank you for saving my life. I wish I could have spoken to you properly, but Paul wouldn't allow it. I don't even know if this note will reach you, but I had to try. I hate lying here with nothing to do but think — about the cave, about the storm, about how little I know of the one who carried me out of both. If you ever want to talk, I'd like that. Maybe when I'm allowed to leave this bed.*
> *Maelis*

I read it once, twice, then a third time, committing every word to memory. Gratitude, yes. But also regret, and a door left open for more. She wanted to talk. To *see* me.

The ache in my chest eased, replaced by a surge of something brighter, fiercer. Hope.

Rainse watched me with a raised brow. "Well? Are you going to smile all night at that scrap of paper, or are you going to tell me what she said?"

I folded the note carefully, reverently, and slid it into the pocket over my heart. "She wishes to see me again."

Rainse chuckled. "Then maybe there's a chance for you after all."

"A chance?" I growled softly. "No. A certainty. She is mine, and one day soon, I will be hers."

"I've asked around the humans - the males, that is. No female is allowed anywhere near one of us finmen. Thanks for that, brother."

I growled again. "Not funny."

"Most of the staff aren't in the Hot Tatties database. They have the option to join, if they want, but most don't. I guess if you work with aliens every day, they don't seem all that exciting and alluring any more. Before you ask, I didn't ask if Maelis joined the dating agency. It would have been too obvious that I was asking on your behalf."

I blew out a long breath, gills fluttering. "You did well. The fewer eyes on her, the better. But that means the agency won't confirm what I already know."

Rainse cocked his head. "So, what are you going to do? Sit here glowering at the walls?"

"No," I said. "I'm going to write to her."

He blinked. "A love letter? In your handwriting? That'll go down well with Paul."

"It doesn't matter what Paul thinks." I went to the small desk by the bed, found a scrap of paper and a stylus. My hands felt too big for the task, but I forced myself to write carefully, each word deliberate:

> *Maelis,*
>
> *I am forbidden to see you, but I cannot stop thinking of you. You are strong and brave and you fought for your life as fiercely as any warrior I have known. I will respect the humans' rules for now because you need rest, but I will not stay away forever. When you are well, if you wish it, I will come to you.*
>
> *Cerban*

I stared at the words until they blurred. Rainse took the note without a word and folded it neatly.

"I'll find a way to get it to her," he said quietly. "No promises, but I'll try."

I gave him a grateful nod. "Thank you, brother."

He shrugged. "She's already changed you. I'm curious to see what happens next."

I straightened, feeling the weight of the situation pressing down on me. "Next, I need to speak with Fionn. He's not just our clutch-brother. He's also our mouthpiece to the humans. If anyone can speak to Pam for me, it's him. But he must hear it from me first — about Maelis, about the cave, about everything. Not what the humans think I did. What actually happened."

"To be fair, I'm amazed he hasn't called you yet," Rainse mused.

"He might be busy with Elise. She wants to show him where she grew up, how she lived before they met."

"I bet she'll delight in showing him her bedroom."

We shared a laugh; the first light moment in way too long.

I followed Rainse into the comms room and he got started at establishing the connection.

"Do you want me to stay for this? Or would you prefer to talk to Fionn alone?" he asked after activating the holo-screen.

"Stay," I said without hesitation. "You're both my clutch-brothers. I want both of your advice and support."

Rainse keyed the comms, and a moment later Fionn's image shimmered into focus. No Elise, no Pam, no humans hovering nearby. Just my clutch-brother, his expression stern but not unkind.

"You've caused a storm louder than the one I heard raged on the island," he said by way of greeting.

Rainse smirked. "He does have a talent for that."

I ignored the jab, stepping closer to the screen. "I wanted to speak with you alone. Without Pam. Without Paul."

Fionn's gaze sharpened. "I know why. You want me to understand what you couldn't say yesterday."

"Yes." My throat felt tight, but the words burned to be spoken. I couldn't delay it with small talk and explanations. "She is my mate."

Fionn didn't flinch. He only nodded slowly, as if he had expected it. "I thought as much. The way you looked when Pam accused you... it wasn't just stubbornness. It was bond."

Rainse leaned back in his chair, folding his arms. "Told you he'd see it."

Fionn shot him a quelling glance before turning back to me. "Tell me everything that happened. Every detail."

And so I did. How I'd talked to her just before the storm. How I'd been worried for her safety. How I'd searched for her beneath the waves. The cave. The desperation. The rescue.

When I was done, Fionn ran a hand through his long hair. "Cerban, it's clear from how you talk about her.

Clear to me and Rainse, probably the other finfolk as well. But not to humans. They don't recognise their mates as we do. And you realise the problem. Without her registered in the database, the agency will never confirm it. Pam will argue you're blinded by infatuation, not instinct. And Paul will use this to push for tighter controls." He growled. "Kelon has a lot to answer for. He destroyed the trust between us and the humans, at least for now. I am doing my best to rebuild it, but that will take time."

"I don't care about their controls," I growled. "I care about Maelis. She would be dead if I had followed their rules. Dead. And I know in my heart she is mine."

Fionn's expression softened. "I believe you, brother. But belief won't protect you from Pam's decisions. What I can do is put my word on record – tell her I recognise the bond, even if the agency refuses to. Coming from me, it may carry weight."

Hope flared, sharp and painful. "You would do that?"

He inclined his head. "Of course. You are my clutch-brother. And maybe Pam will agree to test Maelis, add her DNA to the database to have definite proof. But until then, you must hold steady. Don't break your confinement. Don't give Paul more ammunition. Every misstep will make Pam dig her heels in deeper."

Rainse gave a dry chuckle. "Patience has never been his strongest skill."

"Then he'll have to learn it," Fionn said. His voice softened again, almost a smile tugging at his lips. "For her."

The screen flickered, then dissolved into black.

I stood in the silence, Rainse watching me with that same infuriatingly knowing smirk. My hand strayed to the pocket where her note rested against my chest. My greenskin tightened at the thought of her.

Patience. For her, I would try. But patience alone would never be enough.

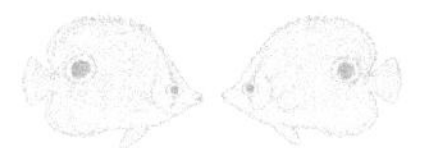

## 11

Maelis

Tyrone brought it in folded neatly, his expression half-exasperated, half-conspiratorial. "Don't ask how it got here," he muttered, sliding the slip of paper onto my blanket. "Just read it before Paul catches me smuggling contraband."

He gave me a wink paired with a concerned frown. We knew this was forbidden. There wouldn't be consequences for me, not really. But I'd had enough time to think about what it would mean for Cerban if it was discovered that he had not gone against the rules yet again. He might be sent back to his home planet, never allowed to return to Earth. The finfolk had come here because on their planet, only a few men got to be with women. Climate change had meant that only a small proportion of the population was female. To get a mate, as they called it, you had to apply and go through vigorous tests - or at least that's what I'd heard. The finmen who'd come to the island had not been allowed to be in a relationship. They'd stay alone for the rest of their lives. The thought made me sad. Some people chose to be single and that was fine until it became a decree imposed on you by others. Everyone deserved a chance of finding love. And if I wasn't careful, Cerban's might be taken away from him for the second time.

The moment Tyrone left, I unfolded the note with hands that trembled more than I liked to admit.

> *Maelis,*
> *I am forbidden to see you, but I cannot stop thinking of you. You are strong and brave and you fought for your life as fiercely as any warrior I have known. I will respect the humans' rules for now because you need rest, but I will not stay away forever. When you are well, if you wish it, I will come to you.*
> *Cerban*

I pressed the paper to my chest, fighting a ridiculous urge to smile. Strong and brave. A warrior. No one had ever written words like that about me before.

Maybe I had judged these aliens prematurely. I did really like him - and not just because he'd saved my life. Not just because he was forbidden.

As much as I wanted to reply, I was also cautious that it would only increase the chance of discovery. If I wrote to him again, it had to be something important, not just a random note professing how much I wanted to see him.

And I had just the thing. I couldn't get the strange rhythm of the bubbles out of my mind.

I'd replayed the footage half a dozen times since yesterday, staring at the steady rise of air against the cave wall. Five bursts. Pause. Five bursts. Pause. Not random. Not natural.

Cerban needed to know. He'd been there, had seen them too – I was certain of it. And if I was right, if those bubbles meant something, then he was the only one who could help me unravel it.

The thought of diving again made my chest tighten. Images of rock crushing down, of the last hiss of my regulator, jolted through me like electric shocks. But the bubbles gave that fear shape, turned it into something I could face. If I could solve their mystery, then the cave wouldn't just be the place I almost died. It would be the place I found answers.

I unfolded his note again, tracing his name with my fingertip. Desperation pressed at me. I had to tell him.

When Tyrone came back to check my vitals, I blurted, "Can you get another message to him?"

He froze, thermometer in hand. "Maelis—"

"Please. Just one. It's not about thank-yous or romance or whatever Pam and Paul think is happening. This is important. I need him to know what I saw down there."

Tyrone sighed, rubbing the bridge of his nose. "You're going to get me fired. Or worse."

But after a moment, he lowered his voice. "Fine. Write it quickly. And keep it vague – I'm not passing along a love letter."

I snatched the paper from the bedside table, words spilling fast, messy but certain:

> Cerban,
> I've been reviewing the dive footage. The bubbles in the cave weren't random. They followed a rhythm: five bursts, pause, five bursts, pause. I need you to help me figure out what it means. When the storm clears, we have to go back. Together.

I folded the paper and pressed it into Tyrone's hand before I could change my mind. "Please."

He shook his head, muttering, "You're both going to kill me," but tucked it into his pocket.

As he left, my pulse quickened. For the first time since

the cave collapse, I felt less like a victim and more like myself again.

If Cerban came back for me – and I had no doubt he would – then the sea hadn't finished with us yet.

I'd just settled back against the pillows, trying to slow the jitter of nerves in my chest, when the door opened again. I expected Tyrone with more tea – or maybe contraband biscuits – but instead Paul strode in. He was dressed sharply in a white suit, the rolled up sleeves the only admission to the tropical climate outside. Now that the storm had passed, the sun was shining again as if nothing had happened.

He looked tired, the storm's aftermath carved into the lines on his face, but his voice was softer than I'd feared.

"Good to see you awake," he said, pulling up the lone chair and sitting rather than looming. "How are you feeling?"

"Like I got run over by a ship," I muttered. "But much better. And alive. Thanks to… him."

Paul nodded, hands clasped loosely between his knees. "Cerban. Yes. I owe him for that. We all do."

The words surprised me. "I thought you were furious."

"I was," he admitted, a faint smile tugging at the corner of his mouth. "Furious at the storm, at the scare you gave us, at the finfolk for breaking rules we can't afford to bend. But not at you. You couldn't have predicted the storm nor the cave collapsing. And Cerban..." He shook his head. "He did the right thing, even if it puts us in a difficult position. None of us knew you were out for a dive, and even if we had, we wouldn't have been able to rescue you."

Relief loosened something tight in my chest. For once, Paul wasn't just the manager reciting rules; he was a man who cared for the people under his watch.

"Pam's been in touch," he went on, his tone turning more businesslike. "You know how she is. She's worried this could undo the trust we've built with the finfolk. She's ordered that Cerban continues to be confined to quarters until she decides what to do."

The thought of Cerban locked away, punished for saving me, made anger prickle beneath my skin. "That's not fair."

Paul gave me a long, steady look. "I don't disagree. But my job is to protect both staff and guests, and sometimes that means keeping to the rules, even when they don't seem fair. What matters now is that you recover. The rest... we'll find a way to handle it."

He stood, smoothing his damp shirt. "Get some rest, Maelis. Tyrone will keep me updated on your progress.

And if you need anything, you come to me. Understood?"

I nodded, the words caught in my throat.

When he left, the room felt quiet again, save for the hiss of the oxygen cylinder. Paul might be bound by rules, but he hadn't condemned Cerban outright. That gave me a sliver of hope that maybe, just maybe, not all bridges were burned quite yet.

12

Cerban

The second sunpass after the storm broke clear and bright, but confinement made it feel no different from the storm itself. I paced my room, the walls closing in, every breath dragging like an anchor. I was so very desperate to get out of here, yet I knew it could destroy everything if I followed that temptation. But ever since Tyrone had smuggled in Maelis' latest message, a note about the bubbles we'd seen in the cave, I'd been re-reading it, committing it to memory. Imagining the female who'd written those words. But also, pondered over the significance of her observations. I was curious to watch her footage. Unless it was different on this planet, no animal or plant would release bubbles at such a regular frequency. But if it wasn't a living thing, what could it be?

What was lurking in that cave, waiting to be discovered?

The door banged open and Rainse strolled in, whistling. He shoved a laundry trolley ahead of him, a pile of blankets spilling over the edges.

"What is this?" I demanded.

"Room service," he said smugly. "Or, more accurately, smuggling service." He gave the trolley a dramatic shake. "Come out before you suffocate."

The blankets stirred and then Maelis pushed herself up, hair tousled, cheeks flushed from the effort of hiding.

For a heartbeat, I could only stare. She looked fragile, yet her eyes shone with stubborn fire and the cuts on her arms were healing well. My mate.

"Surprise," she said, slightly breathless.

I crossed the room in two strides and caught her before she could stumble out of the trolley, steadying her against me. "You should be in bed."

"And miss this?" She tilted her chin up, defiant. "Not a chance. Besides, I had something important to tell you."

Rainse cleared his throat. "I will give you some time together. Knock on the wall when you need me. And brother... don't do anything stupid."

She reached into her pocket and pulled out the little camera housing. "The bubbles. They weren't random, Cerban. They pulsed in a pattern. Five bursts, then a pause. Over and over. Look."

She showed me the grainy footage, and there it was: the rhythm, steady as a drumbeat.

I felt the hair along my arms rise, my gills flaring with the memory of their metallic tang. "I saw them too. I thought... later. But later never came."

Her eyes met mine, fierce and bright. "Then we have to go back. Whatever made those bubbles – it's not natural. It means something."

The words lit a spark in her, but in me they ignited only fear. I tightened my grip on her hand, perhaps too much, because she winced. "No. Never again. That cave almost killed you. I will not take you back there."

Her mouth opened, then snapped shut. She pulled her hand free, anger sparking in her gaze. "You don't get to decide that for me."

"I dragged you out of there half-dead," I said sharply. "Your tank empty, your body limp. I won't see that happen again."

Maelis bristled, the fragile flush of her cheeks belying the steel in her voice. "It nearly killed me, yes. But it also gave me purpose. If I can understand the bubbles, then that cave isn't just where I almost died. It's where I found something bigger. Don't you see? It's not just fear – it's a mystery worth solving."

I dragged a hand through my hair, frustration tightening every muscle. She was fragile, human, still recovering. Yet she stood there, fire in her eyes, ready to dive back into the very place I dreaded most.

"Cerban." Maelis's voice softened, steady but no less determined. "You saved my life. But I'm not a child. I won't spend the rest of my time here afraid of the water. And I won't ignore what I saw down there."

I closed my eyes, torn between instinct and reason, between my need to shield her and her need to seek answers.

One thing was certain: I wouldn't let her face it alone, no matter what I said now.

When I opened them again, she was watching me, her expression unreadable.

"Why do you care so much?" she asked quietly. "I mean – yes, you saved me. But this is more than duty, isn't it? You're... different with me."

Her words struck like a harpoon. If she knew the truth – that every beat of my heart now throbbed in time with hers, that my greenskin would always guide me to wherever she was in the world, no, the universe – what then? She wasn't ready to hear it. Not yet.

I stepped closer, fighting the urge to take her into my arms. "You were dying in my arms, Maelis. Do you think anyone could walk away from that unchanged?"

Her breath caught. She tilted her chin up, and the defiance in her dark eyes melted into something softer, something dangerous. "Maybe. Or maybe you're just saying that to make me feel special."

"I don't say what I don't mean." My voice was low, rougher than I intended.

We stood close enough that her scent – salt and florals and home – wrapped around me like the tide. My hand itched to touch her, to trace the line of her jaw, to remind myself she was real and alive.

For a moment, neither of us moved. Her lips parted ever so slightly, her gaze flicking down to my mouth before darting back up again. The air between us thickened. A storm was brewing and this time, it wasn't happening on the outside.

Then she stepped back, the spell breaking. "This... whatever this is... it can't happen, can it? Paul, Pam, the rules – they'd never allow it."

The distance cut sharper than any blade, but I forced myself to stay still. "Rules are fragile things. They can be broken."

She gave a shaky laugh. "You really don't make this easy."

Her laugh faded, leaving only the steady thud of her pulse, quick and unsteady. She didn't step further away. Instead, she lingered there in the charged space between us, eyes locked on mine.

I moved before I thought better of it, closing the last inches. My hand rose, fingers brushing a damp strand of hair from her cheek. Her skin was warm beneath my touch, fragile and alive in a way that made my chest ache.

She drew in a sharp breath but didn't pull back. Her gaze dropped to my mouth, lingered there, then flicked up again.

The world narrowed to this – her lips, parted slightly, the faint tremor of her breath, the pounding of her heart so loud I could almost hear it.

I bent lower, close enough that the heat of her breath mingled with mine. Her eyes fluttered shut–

"Careful, brother," Rainse's voice drawled from the doorway.

Maelis jerked back, cheeks flushing crimson. My hand dropped to my side, my claws flexing in frustration.

Rainse pointed at the trolley. "Some human staff is on the way here, they want to clean the room. Maelis, you better get back."

She nodded quickly, though her wide eyes flicked to mine before she moved. I caught the tremor in her hands as she tugged the blanket pile aside and climbed back into the trolley.

I wanted to stop her. To pull her back, finish what had been interrupted. To hear the sound of her saying my name when our mouths finally met.

But Rainse was right. If anyone else saw her here, it wouldn't just be trouble, it would be disaster.

She settled into the hollow, pulling a corner of blanket over her face. Only her eyes showed, glinting in the dim light. "Don't... don't forget what we talked about," she whispered.

My heart slammed once, twice. "I won't."

Rainse snapped the trolley's cover into place and shoved it toward the door. "I'll get her back without anyone noticing. Try not to do anything stupid while I'm gone, brother."

"Too late for that," I muttered.

Maelis's gaze met mine one last time before the blankets hid her from sight. Then Rainse wheeled her out, whistling as though he really was only carting laundry.

The door closed, and I stood in the silence, claws flexing uselessly, breath still uneven. The ghost of her warmth lingered on my fingers, her scent in my lungs, the almost-kiss hanging between us like the pull of a current too strong to fight.

No matter what Pam or Paul decreed, no matter the threat of chains and exile. I would not let them keep her from me.

Maelis

It was good to be back in my own apartment. Tyrone had scheduled a follow-up appointment for tomorrow, but for now, I was free to do whatever I pleased. Paul had explicitly forbidden me from working for the rest of the week. Enjoy the island, he'd said. But what I really wanted was to dive *below* the island once again.

The thought made my stomach twist. Every time I closed my eyes, I could still feel the crush of the cave walls, the rasp of stone against my tank, the hiss of dwindling air. Panic crept in like cold water seeping through a crack.

And yet, stronger than fear, was curiosity. Those bubbles. The rhythm. The pattern that refused to leave me alone. I'd seen plenty of strange things under the sea – schools of fish forming spirals, coral shifting with the current, even volcanic vents releasing bursts of steam – but nothing that precise.

I stretched out on the bed, staring at the ceiling fan as it lazily turned. The room smelled of salt and sun-baked wood. My wetsuit and fins leaned against the wall where I'd dropped them in a heap. For the first time in days, the space felt... mine. Safe.

But it was an illusion. Because somewhere across the resort, Cerban was locked away, punished for saving me. The memory of his hand brushing my cheek, the heat of his breath against mine – too close, too dangerous – burned fresh across my skin.

I pressed my palms to my face and groaned. What was I doing? He was an alien warrior. A guest, not a staff member. Someone I wasn't supposed to look at for more than a few seconds, let alone...

Yet I couldn't stop thinking about him. About the way his eyes had looked in the dimness, fierce and unyielding, but soft when they rested on me. About how my body had leaned toward his as if pulled by the tide itself.

I rolled onto my side, glaring at the crumpled camera housing on the nightstand. "Damn bubbles," I muttered.

Because the mystery of the cave was the only excuse I had left. If I could focus on that, if I could convince myself this pull toward Cerban was about science, discovery, purpose – then maybe I could ignore the truth humming in my chest whenever I thought of him.

*Maybe.*

I pushed myself upright, restless energy prickling through me. I'd promised Tyrone and Paul I'd rest, but lying here only made me more aware of what I wasn't doing. The cave was out there, waiting. The bubbles were out there.

And I wasn't the type to sit around and wait for answers to fall into my lap.

Crossing the small room, I pulled my gear bag onto the bed and started sorting through it. My wetsuit was still damp from its hurried retrieval, but that didn't matter. What mattered was that I'd learned from last time.

One tank hadn't been enough. I'd been careless, too eager to push deeper without accounting for the unknown. That mistake had nearly cost me my life.

So: spare cylinders. I jotted a quick mental checklist, the way I did when preparing dives for paying clients. Two primary tanks. One stage cylinder, clipped to my harness for emergencies. Backup lights. Redundant reels and line.

The routine of preparing for a dive steadied me, pushed away the dark memories. I could do this.

I *had* to do this.

And I wouldn't go alone this time.

I swallowed hard, because I already knew who I wanted at my side. The same person who'd dragged me out alive, who'd held me against his chest when I thought the sea had claimed me. Cerban.

Even thinking his name made my pulse quicken. But I shook the distraction off and focused on the gear.

We'd never managed to continue our discussion about returning to the cave. Rainse had interrupted us. And both Rainse and Tyrone had made it very clear that they would not be carrying messages back and forth between us again. They were trying to protect us, I knew that, but I hated not being able to talk to Cerban.

Wait. I was an idiot. I almost slammed my head against my forehead at my sheer stupidity. Of course I could talk to him, now that I was back in my own place. This wasn't the eighteenth century where people had to rely on letters to talk to each other. There was such a thing as a phone. And because this was a fancy resort, every room had not just a phone, but an entire videocall system - including staff apartments. I smiled to myself and searched for the aliens' accommodation in the directory.

My finger hovered over the call button, my heart hammering.

This was ridiculous. I'd faced sharks with less nerves than I had for this.

Before I could chicken out, I tapped the screen. The ring tone pulsed softly in my little apartment, echoing like a sonar ping.

After three beats, the feed flickered to life. Cerban appeared, shoulders filling the frame, his face shadowed but unmistakably him. His gills fluttered once, then stilled.

"Maelis," he said, low and rough.

"Hi," I managed, trying to sound casual even as my heart leapt. "Sorry to... surprise you. I realised I could just call."

For a moment he only looked at me, as though memorising my face. Then, softly: "I am glad you did."

Heat rushed to my cheeks. "I'm... back in my apartment. Tyrone says I'm fine. Paul gave me the week off."

"I know," he said. "Rainse told me."

I fiddled with the edge of my wetsuit. "I can't stop thinking about the bubbles."

His expression darkened slightly. "Maelis–"

"No, listen." I leaned closer to the screen, urgency creeping into my voice. "I'm not asking you to watch me nearly drown again. I've made a checklist. Spare cylinders, backup lights, emergency lines. I'll be prepared this time. But I can't do this without you."

"It is not just danger. I'm not supposed to leave this building, let alone go for a dive with you. If we're discovered... it won't end well."

"I know," I said quietly. I knew what I was asking of him. "But... something is drawing me back to that cave. I can't explain it. I need to go back. I need to know what these bubbles mean. What causes them.

Don't you want to know what made them?"

His gills fluttered once, his jaw tight.

"I want to know," he admitted at last. "But I want you safe more."

I hesitated, then pressed my hand to the screen as if I could reach through to him. "Then come with me. Help me make it safe. Together."

For a long moment he didn't move. Then his massive hand lifted, mirroring mine from the other side of the glass. "You are stubborn," he murmured.

"Occupational hazard," I said with a weak smile. "Dive instructor."

The corner of his mouth twitched, quickly suppressed. "Very well. We will plan. Carefully. No one must know."

Relief loosened something tight in my chest. "Thank you."

He leaned closer, voice a low rumble that seemed to vibrate through the connection. "But if anything happens, Maelis... I will not forgive myself."

I swallowed hard, pulse racing. "Then we'll make sure nothing does."

We stared at each other, the air between us charged even through a screen. The cave, the bubbles, the rules – all of it waited beneath the surface. But for the first time, it felt like something we'd face together.

"I'll bring spare cylinders this time," I said quickly when he didn't reply. "Backup lights, reels, everything. I won't make the same mistake twice."

"You should not have made it once," he countered, but there was no real anger in his voice – only the rasp of fear still lingering in him.

I lifted my chin. "That's why you'll be with me. We do this carefully. No risks we don't account for."

His eyes narrowed slightly, weighing me the way a commander weighs the readiness of a warrior. At last, he nodded. "Dawn. Fewer eyes watching then. Rainse can cover for us."

Silence stretched between us again, heavy but not uncomfortable. My fingers itched to reach for him, though all I had was a screen.

"Maelis." His voice was low, hesitant in a way I hadn't

heard before. "When you are with me under the water... stay close. Always. Promise me this."

"I promise," I whispered.

His shoulders lowered as though a weight had lifted, though his gaze was still fierce, still protective. "Then we will see what the sea is hiding."

The line clicked softly, the call ending before I could say anything more.

I stared at my reflection on the darkened screen, heart pounding, gear still spread across the bed. Suddenly, I didn't feel like the woman who had almost died in the dark deep.

I felt like someone about to discover something extraordinary.

14

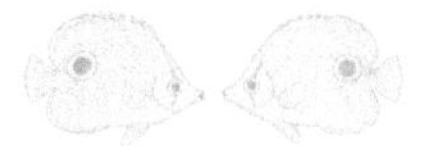

Cerban

Sneaking out of the accommodation block had been easier than I could have hoped for. And it had totally been worth the look on Maelis' face when she'd spotted me waiting outside her diving shack.

The planet's sun had barely breached the horizon as we waded into the water, a sea so calm it looked like an entirely different ocean. The chaos of the storm had scrubbed the shore clean, leaving behind sand as smooth as glass and a silence broken only by the rhythm of the waves.

Maelis adjusted the straps of her gear with brisk efficiency, her movements sharp but steady. She'd doubled her tanks this time, checked every gauge twice. Her determination glowed brighter than the rising light.

Still, my chest tightened. I remembered her limp body in my arms, the way her breath had faltered, and every instinct in me screamed that bringing her back here was madness.

Yet when she caught me watching, her lips curved in a small, wry smile. "Don't look at me like I'm about to break. I'm fine."

"You nearly died." My voice was low, rougher than I meant.

She tugged her mask into place, her eyes never leaving mine. "That's why you're here, isn't it?"

I swallowed hard. She wasn't wrong. I was here because I couldn't let her out of my sight. Because the thought of her facing the sea without me was unbearable.

She hesitated, then reached for my hand. "Wait. Before we go under, you need to know this."

I raised a brow. "I know how to swim."

She gave me a look sharp enough to slice kelp. "Not swim. *Communicate.* I know you can talk underwater, but I can't." She lifted her hand, fingers curled into a fist. "This means low on air." Then she pressed the heel of her palm flat against her throat. "Out of air. Emergency."

I watched carefully, committing each movement to memory.

She pointed two fingers at her eyes, then toward me. "This means I'm watching you."

A faint smile tugged at my lips. "You will be watching me?"

Colour flushed her cheeks, but she didn't back down. "Yes. And this—" she made a circle with her thumb and forefinger, the other three fingers extended – "means okay. If you see me do this, I'm fine. If I *don't* do it back, I'm not."

I copied the gesture, my larger hand dwarfing hers. "Like this?"

"Exactly." For the first time since the storm, she smiled – small but genuine. "Good student."

Her praise stirred something warm in my chest, stronger than the dawn light. I tightened the straps across my chest and adjusted my regulator. "Stay close," I told her.

She rolled her eyes, but the faint quirk of her lips betrayed her amusement. "You already made me promise."

We slipped beneath the surface together, the world shifting instantly from air to water, silence to song. Currents whispered against my skin, fish darted from our approach, and the reef stretched ahead like a sleeping giant waiting to be explored.

She swam with strong, confident strokes, her light cutting through the dim water. But even with her training, even with the new gear, I stayed close enough to feel the brush of her bubbles across my skin.

Because this time, if the sea tried to take her again, it would have to take me too.

We slipped beneath the surface together, the world shifting instantly from air to water. Currents whispered against my greenskin, fish darted from our approach, and the reef stretched ahead like a sleeping giant waiting to be explored. My gills drew in cold water, filtering out the oxygen. My entire body relaxed as I was home. I could live on land, but it would never feel as good as *this*.

Maelis swam with strong, confident strokes, her light cutting through the dim water. But even with her training, even with the extra gear, I stayed close enough to feel the brush of her bubbles across my skin. Just in case.

The sea was calm after the storm, the water clear as glass. Schools of fish glittered like falling stars, weaving in and out of the coral. She paused now and again to shine her torch into crevices, eyes bright with excitement behind her mask. I loved seeing her like this. So full of life.

I followed her gaze to a hollow where a creature stirred. An eight-armed flabby sort of beast, its body shifting colours as it flowed out into the open. First pale, then dark, then rippling in patterns of bronze and green that reminded me of home. I would have loved to ask Maelis what it was called, but I knew she wouldn't have been able to respond. It was unfair to speak when she could not.

She froze as she spotted the creature, holding up a hand to halt me. She hovered perfectly still, only the gentle flick of her fins keeping her suspended. Her reverence was palpable even through the water.

The creature regarded us for a long moment, its intelligent eyes reflecting the beam of her torch. Then, with a graceful unfurling of arms, it spread wide, drifting like a ghost across the sand before disappearing into another crevice.

Maelis turned to me, her eyes wide with delight. She tapped her fingers against her mask in the gesture she'd shown me – *watching you* – and then formed the round circle with her thumb and finger. *Okay.*

I returned the gesture, though what I really wanted was to pull her close, to press my forehead to hers and tell her she was more beautiful than anything in the ocean.

Instead, I swam at her side as she angled her body downward, toward the shadowed drop where the reef gave way to the cliff face. The cave waited below, a darkness cut into the rock.

The calm of the reef faded with every metre of descent. Here, the water was colder, still touched by the storm's aftermath. Sand drifted up in lazy clouds, obscuring the jagged cracks and crevices.

My gills flared as the current shifted. The ocean was restless here. I tasted metal on the water.

The cave was near.

The cliff face loomed, dark and jagged, its surface scarred by cracks that reached down into the gloom. Maelis slowed, her torch beam sweeping back and forth, deliberate now. I matched her pace, every sense alert.

Then I saw them.

Bubbles, faint but unmistakable, trickling from a narrow seam in the rock. They spiralled upward in silvery threads, catching the light like strands of glass.

I tasted them against my gills and shivered. Not plant gas. Not volcanic vent. Something else.

Maelis pointed sharply, excitement vibrating through her whole body. She hovered in front of the seam, her gaze locked on the tiny streams.

We stayed there, watching.

One... two... three... four... five bursts. Pause. One... two... three... four... five.

The rhythm was the same as before. Steady. Intentional. Too precise to be anything but deliberate.

Maelis turned to me, her eyes wide behind the mask, and tapped the *okay* sign, then jabbed her finger toward the bubbles as if to say, *Do you see it?*

I nodded once, slowly, then mimicked her gesture back. *Yes.*

We hovered in the water, silent witnesses to the sea's secret song. The bubbles pulsed on, as though the cave itself was breathing.

My chest tightened. Whatever lay beyond that seam, it was no natural formation. It was waiting. Calling. And I knew, with a certainty that dug deep into my bones, that if we followed those bubbles, we would not return unchanged.

Something caught my eye, further to the right. More bubbles, separate from the main group.

They rose from a lower crevice, faint at first, curling through the current.

I frowned. That fissure hadn't been there before. I was certain of it.

The water here carried the taste of new stone – raw, unsettled. The storm must have shifted part of the cliff face, peeling back a layer that had hidden the opening before. A natural disguise, or perhaps not so natural.

I gestured to Maelis, drawing her attention to the spot. She angled her torch toward it, and as the beam cut through the haze, the water shimmered strangely, as though light bent around the crevice itself.

A shimmer like that didn't belong in a geological formation.

Maelis's eyes widened behind her mask.

"The storm must have uncovered it," I said aloud, breaking the silence.

She nodded and watched the bubbles.

Five bursts. Pause. Five bursts.

Up close, I could see faint traces along the stone — smooth lines too regular for erosion, like something once sealed the passage shut. My skin prickled with the memory of finfolk architecture: the fluid patterns, the deliberate symmetry. This was something familiar - but how? I knew my ancestors had crash-landed on Earth many generations ago, but the story of Jonet and Ma'vel had taken place in a country called Scotland, far to the east of here. I hadn't realised the finfolk had spread across the planet's oceans before they'd been rescued and brought home to Finfolkaheem.

Maelis reached out and ran a gloved hand along the edge of the opening. The moment she did, the shimmer flickered again – like static beneath the surface – and then vanished. The bubbles thickened, streaming past us in perfect synchrony.

We froze, waiting for the water to settle. When it didn't, she turned to me, her expression unreadable. She pointed at the entrance as if to ask, *Go in?*

Every instinct screamed *no*, but I also knew that whatever secret the storm had unearthed, this was the only way to find it. And Maelis needed this. She needed closure.

I gave a sharp nod. "Slowly."

Maelis went first, her fins stirring a trail of silver bubbles that curled after her like smoke. I followed, one hand brushing the smooth stone, half expecting it to spark under my touch. My greenskin was tight, my muscles ready to jump into action. This could be a trap.

The dark passage narrowed so much that stone scraped against my skin as I squeezed through, then opened suddenly into a chamber that took my breath away.

Light flickered faintly along the walls – not from Maelis' torch, but from veins of metal threaded through the rock. They glowed with a pulse that matched the rhythm of the bubbles. I felt the vibration hum through my bones, through the water, through my very blood.

This was no ordinary cave.

It was something built.

And whatever it was, it had been sleeping here for a very long time.

15

Maelis

For a moment, I could only stare.

The chamber wasn't large, but it felt alive. The walls shimmered faintly, veins of silvery metal threading through the stone like roots. Bubbles drifted upward in steady bursts, their rhythm echoing softly in my chest.

And in the centre of it all was the source.

A sphere – half metal, half coral – sat embedded in the cave floor. It was the size of a boulder, its surface smooth and curved except where living coral had fused into it, spiralling upward in delicate ridges. Light pulsed faintly within, the same rhythm as the bubbles.

It was breathing.

I drifted closer, torchlight sliding across the strange surface. The metallic parts gleamed with a dull, opalescent sheen, but the coral was translucent, its tendrils pulsing with faint bioluminescent light. The whole thing gave off a quiet hum, like the soft thrum of an engine – or a heartbeat.

Cerban was by my side, a protective, cautious presence. I knew letting me enter the cave first had to have been difficult for him. I'd tell him later how much I appreciated it. I was jealous of his ability to talk underwater. Right now, I would have loved to discuss what stood before us.

I couldn't look away. This wasn't just geology or biology. It was both, merged into something utterly alien.

I reached out a hand before I could think better of it.

But this time, Cerban stopped me, his fingers clasping around my wrist.

"Don't. I think I know what this is. Let me."

I was very tempted to ignore him, but this thing was clearly not of human origin, so I had to admit that Cerban likely knew more about it than me.

He carefully pressed a hand to the top of the sphere, then moved it in a figure of eight shape, slowly and with purpose. The flow of bubbles ceased. It was as if the cave was holding its breath, waiting for what was to come.

"There!" Cerban exclaimed with a jubilant grin. "I was right."

A circle of symbols appeared on the sphere's metal surface, glowing softly. They made no sense to me, but Cerban studied them intently. He touched one - and suddenly the cave was drenched in fluorescent light, illuminating every crevice, every pebble on the floor.

"This language is not one I can read or speak, but it still makes sense to me," he explained. "It must be related to our modern language. And this symbol... yes, that will make things easier."

He touched another part of the sphere. A host of bubbles rose from where coral met metal, small ones first, then larger ones. A silver film covered the sphere - no, not silver. It was air. The bubble expanded, beyond the machine, growing fast. I flinched when it reached me, but then cool, dry air kissed my skin, and I froze in astonishment. Water was being pushed out of the cave. I sank to the ground, no longer swimming.

It only took a few seconds for the air bubble to fill the entire room. I stared at Cerban, who was just as wide-eyed as I must have looked. I pointed at my regulator.

His gills fluttered for a moment as he tested the air, then he breathed in deep through his mouth. "It's safe. The oxygen concentration is very much like it is on the surface. You can remove your breathing equipment, but I would keep it close by. I'm not sure how long this will last."

I gingerly took the regulator from my mouth, then yawned and pursed my lips, stretching my mouth muscles. The air smelled a little metallic, but it was barely noticeable.

"What's happening?" I asked. My voice echoed through the cave.

"This device seems like an early version of those we use back on Finfolkaheem to create air rooms underwater. While many finfolk prefer to live in water at all times, some like to have parts of their homes filled with air. Some farming is done on the surface or in huge air domes on the ocean floor. Half of the chambers in the Archives, where Fionn used to work, are air rooms, to protect artefacts that would not survive in water."

I looked around me, searching for anything that looked different now that the water had disappeared.

"Why is it in this cave? Is there something that needs air?"

"I don't know," Cerban admitted. "But this is not the device's only function. I think this symbol... yes."

Turquoise light rippled outward from the core, racing along the metallic veins in the walls until the entire chamber glowed.

Shapes appeared within the light. Faint, ghostlike projections that shimmered in the water like memories caught in a dream. I blinked hard, heart pounding.

Figures.

Two of them. A tall, broad form with long fins trailing from his arms and back – finfolk. And beside him, smaller, with flowing hair and human limbs. They swam close together, hands entwined.

I forgot to breathe.

The vision flickered, the light dimming before flaring again – this time showing more of them. Dozens of pairs, finfolk and humans walking side by side through air-filled halls, their movements graceful, familiar, harmonious.

I turned slowly, trying to take it all in. The images danced along the walls, accompanied by a low, resonant hum that I felt in my bones.

"It's a memory orb," Cerban whispered. "I've only ever heard whispers of them. I did not expect to find one here."

The words sent a shiver through me. "A what?"

He crouched beside the sphere, his fingers tracing one of the glowing symbols. "They were used by my ancestors – long before the first archives were built – to store memories and history. But this one... this one is far older than anything I've ever seen."

The light flared again, brighter now. The figures moved, becoming clearer, more detailed. Their faces were distinct: finfolk and humans, working side by side, speaking, laughing. One scene showed them planting coral together, the living structures weaving themselves into elegant arches. Another showed them gathering beneath a vast dome of glass and water, their reflections mingling on the surface.

The longer I watched, the harder it was to breathe. This wasn't just evidence – it was proof. Proof that humans and finfolk hadn't just met before; they'd *lived together*.

"When Fionn found those records," Cerban muttered, almost to himself. "We thought Ma'vel and Jonet had been an anomaly. A finfolk-human couple, getting together despite the odds. But this... This is proof that they weren't alone. Other unions between the two species happened. Here, far away from Scotland. And look - is that a fingirl?"

I followed his gaze. A child was sitting at the feet of a human woman, a girl with webbed feet and gills, but her greenskin was shorter than usual and her skin was the pale pink of a human.

"A hybrid," I whispered. "They were able to have children together."

"Just like Jonet and Ma'vel. I have been wondering if their offspring was a miracle. This shows that it was not." He sucked in a deep breath. "It feels like a dream, Maelis."

His voice trembled slightly. I found myself reaching out, putting a hand on his shoulder.

"Maybe it's not a dream. Maybe it's a memory your people forgot."

He turned to look at me. The turquoise light rippled across his face, softening the sharpness of his features. "If this is true... Then there is hope. Not just for my clutch-brothers and me, but all finmen. We came here to find mates, to fulfil that yearning to not be alone any longer - but we didn't dare to hope. When Fionn found Elise, we all rejoiced for him, of course, but there was still that lingering doubt. What if it was rare to find a mate among humans? What if he would be the only one?" Cerban smiled slightly. "This is hope for my species, Maelis, but I don't need it. I already know that my mate is on this planet. I don't need a dating agency or an ancient artefact to tell me."

My skin grew cold suddenly. He had a mate. Somewhere on Earth. He'd find her, either with the help of the Hot Tatties or by some other means. And then he'd be gone, with her, and I'd be-

What? Alone? I liked being single. I had been a long time now. I loved my independence. I loved that I could quit my job any time I wanted to and move elsewhere, without having to think about others. I loved that I could decide what to watch on TV at night, without having to compromise. I loved to starfish in my double bed, lying diagonally on the mattress. I loved...

Him.

The thought hit me like a current, sudden and unrelenting. My heart stuttered, and for a moment I forgot how to breathe. I'd known it, somewhere deep down, since the first time I saw him on the beach, water gleaming on his skin. But saying it – even to myself – was dangerous. Reckless.

I dropped my hand from his shoulder before he could notice the tremor in it. "That's... wonderful, Cerban," I managed, my voice barely more than a whisper. "I'm happy for you."

He frowned slightly, the faintest crease forming between his brows. "You do not sound happy."

"I'm just..." I gestured vaguely at the orb, desperate for a distraction. "Overwhelmed, I suppose. This is huge, isn't it? You're standing in front of proof that everything your people thought was lost might still exist. That's – well – it's a lot."

His gaze lingered on me, sharp and searching, but then he nodded slowly. "It is," he said softly. "And yet, the only thing I can think of is how right it feels to be here. With you."

The air between us thickened. My heart stumbled again. He shouldn't say stuff like that. Not when another woman was out there, somewhere, destined for him.

I took a small step back, needing space but finding none. The cave suddenly felt too small, the air too heavy. "We should record everything," I said quickly, crouching to reach for my camera. "We'll need evidence for Paul and the others. If this orb can create air, we can bring instruments down safely, get proper footage–"

"Maelis." His voice stopped me, low and steady. "You are shaking."

"I'm fine," I lied, even as my hands trembled over the camera housing. "Just cold."

He stepped closer. "You are not cold. You are frightened."

I looked up sharply, ready to deny it, but the words caught in my throat. Not because he was wrong – but because it wasn't the cave, or the memory orb, or the strange, ancient light that scared me.

It was him. What I felt when he looked at me like that. What it meant.

"I'm not afraid of you," I said quietly.

His eyes bored into me. "Then what are you scared of?"

I couldn't tell him. It was too embarrassing. Too cruel. I knew how desperate he and his kind were. I should be happy for him. Delighted, even. But I was not a good person. I couldn't give him my happiness, nor the unknown woman.

Actually, I was a terrible person. Because I despised her. Hoped he'd never meet her. Wished her all sorts of bad things.

Because I was selfish.

I wanted him.

I forced myself to move. "We should go. The air won't last forever."

He nodded, but there was something unreadable in his expression as he turned back to the sphere, running one last hand across its glowing surface. The symbols dimmed at his touch, and the hum softened until it was barely audible.

As we packed our gear and prepared to leave, I couldn't stop glancing back. The orb seemed to watch us, its faint light following our movements.

Was it judging me? Or would it give me its blessing if I fought for what was mine?

16

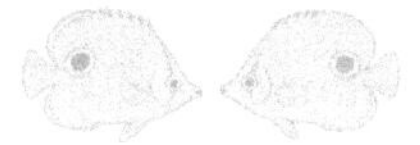

Cerban

Something was wrong. The water between us felt cold and heavy. She avoided my gaze, only making the most basic necessary dive gestures, as we ascended slowly. This time, I made sure to take breaks. I didn't want her to become unwell again.

When we finally broke the surface, sunlight splintered across the waves. Maelis lifted her mask and squinted toward shore. A few figures were waiting by the waterline – Paul, Tyrone, and two other staff members. They were watching us, arms folded, tension visible even from here.

Maelis gave a brief wave. "We're fine!" she called, her voice rough from the regulator.

Paul didn't look convinced. He stepped into the shallows as we approached, hands on his hips. "You were supposed to rest, Maelis," he said tightly. "And you—" he shot me a glare "—were supposed to stay away from her."

"We found something important," she said evenly before I could defend myself. "Something the finmen and the agency will want to see."

"Not the point," Paul snapped. "You risked both your lives. Again."

Maelis stripped off her fins, water streaming down her hair and wetsuit. "I knew what I was doing, Paul. We both did."

"Again, not the point. Cerban, I talked to Pam when I discovered that both of you were missing. She's decided that you cannot stay on Earth. She will be contacting the Intergalactic Authority to arrange an official ban and to organise transport to your planet."

My blood froze. I couldn't breathe.

Banished. Taken away from her. Forever. For a finman, being separated from his mate was worse than death.

"You... you can't do that," I gasped.

Paul's glare was icy. "You have been warned repeatedly. You ignored the rules. Ignored your punishment. You seem to think that we are beneath you and that you can do whatever you want. Well, you are wrong. You-"

He was distracted by someone running along the beach. I recognised him right away. Rainse.

His presence gave me strength. Heat rose through me, not just anger but something deeper, more primal. I stepped forward, the water surging against my greenskin. "I will not go."

Paul's eyes narrowed. "You don't have a choice."

"I do." My voice deepened, carrying over the wind. "I will not leave her."

Maelis blinked at me. "Cerban, you said you have a-"

"She is mine," I said, the words erupting from somewhere I couldn't suppress any longer. "Maelis is my mate."

Everything stopped.

The waves lapped at the sand. My brother came to a stop, breathless and flustered. Tyrone dropped the pen he'd been holding. Paul stared at me, stunned into silence.

And Maelis... Maelis went very still, as though the entire world had narrowed to the space between us.

"I..." she breathed, her voice faint. "What did you just say?"

"I said," I repeated more softly now, my voice shaking with the force of it, "you are my mate."

Everything around us faded away. I didn't care that we had an audience. Nothing mattered but Maelis.

"But..." she whispered. "You..." And slowly, understanding dawned on her face. "You didn't mean another woman when you talked about your mate on this planet. You already knew. You knew it was me. How? I never took a test. I'm not in the dating agency's database."

I placed my hands on my chest, right above my heart. "I knew it from the first moment I saw you. It just took a while for me to truly understand what I was feeling."

Maelis lifted a trembling hand to her mouth. She looked like someone who'd stepped off a cliff and only now realised she was flying.

"Are you sure?" she asked, just loud enough for me to hear.

"With every fibre of my being. Every drop of water in me is being pulled towards you, Maelis. You are my moon. My sun. My everything. And I am sorry I did not tell you before."

Maelis's eyes searched mine, full of confusion, disbelief... and something that looked a lot like hope. "Cerban..."

I didn't plan to move closer, but I did. The world shrank until there was nothing but her – the curve of her mouth, the salt clinging to her skin, the way the sunlight caught in her wet hair.

"Tell me you don't feel it," I murmured. "And I'll never touch you again."

She opened her mouth as if to argue, but no sound came out. Then she stepped into me, her hands pulling at the damp wrap around my waist.

And just like that, she was kissing me.

The sea roared behind us, warm air wrapping around our bodies as though the island itself was holding its breath. Her lips were soft and determined, tasting of salt and courage. I cupped her face, deepening the kiss, feeling the bond flare between us like sunlight breaking through deep water.

Someone cleared their throat loudly.

We broke apart, both of us breathless. Paul stood a few metres away, jaw tight. "That's enough," he said stiffly. "Inside. Now."

They let Maelis get changed before they herded us back to the main resort buildings. I would have liked for her to get some rest, have some food and refreshments, but it wasn't to be.

A screen flickered to life on the far wall – Pam's face appeared, composed but strained.

"You again," she said with a sigh. "You'd think I have nothing else to do than deal with a rule-averse finman and a diver who keeps going missing. What have you two done this time? Where did you go?"

Maelis and I exchanged a look. Was this the time to tell her about the finfolk artefact hidden in the cave? It felt wrong. I should talk to my brothers first, then the other finmen, before involving the humans. She gave me a small nod as if to say that she'd follow my lead in this.

"Maelis wanted to return to the cave," I began. "So I offered to join her for protection."

"Yes, I needed to face my fears," Maelis added quickly. "I'd had nightmares about what happened down there. I had to go back to process everything. And I knew that going by myself would have been foolish, so I involved Cerban. I know he wasn't supposed to-"

Paul interrupted her. "He was supposed to be in his quarters, far away from you and other women. Kelon proved just how unpredictable finmen can be."

"I am not Kelon," I hissed. "I am nothing like him. Don't you humans have rotten shells among your pearls? Do not judge me by another male's actions."

Pam sighed again. "I hear what you're saying, but you have to understand that we have to stand firm on certain principles, especially after the IA got involved. All you had to do was stay in your room until the dust had settled. Cerban, what in the stars were you thinking?"

"I was thinking that I will not be separated from my *mate*," I said, voice steady.

Pam's eyes widened as she realised what I'd just said, but then her expression hardened again. She pinched the bridge of her nose. "Your mate? You can't just *declare* that, Cerban, and think that this will solve everything. You know the regulations. Human matches must be verified. Especially with your history."

"I don't care about regulations," I growled. "I know what I feel."

Maelis stepped forward. "Then test us," she said. "You said yourself the bond can be proven. Take my DNA, take his – whatever you need. Just don't send him away until you know for sure."

Pam's gaze softened. "Very well. Paul, take samples from Maelis. Cerban is already in the database. I'll rush the results through the lab. But until we know the outcome, Cerban is to be confined to the finmen quarters. No more excursions. No more running away. And as soon as Fionn gets back to the island, you'll be staying on the spaceship. Shall I inform him of today's events, or will you?"

"I will call him," Rainse offered. "I have a feeling that we should have a clutch-brothers meeting. Just the three of us."

Pam nodded. "Good. Stay out of trouble, all of you. Or I shall remove every single finman from the Hot Tatties database."

The screen went dark.

Paul rubbed his temples. "All right. Let's get this over with." He handed Maelis a sterile swab. She rubbed it against the inside of her cheek in slow, almost meditative movements. What was she thinking? Was she doubting our connection? Or hoping that this would prove it to the rest of the world?

When Paul sealed the sample in a plastic tube, he looked exhausted. "Cerban, time for you to return to your quarters. I'll have someone escort you back."

"I don't need an escort," I said.

Maelis stepped forward. "I will take him."

Paul gaped at her. "You? That's-"

"Pam didn't say anything about Cerban having to be by himself while he's confined to his room. Please give us some privacy."

And with that, she took my hand and led me out of the room.

If I hadn't loved her already, I would have fallen for her that very moment. Hard.

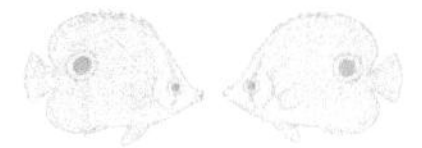

## 17

Maelis

My palm was damp against his – part seawater, part nerves – but I didn't let go. My fingers tightened around Cerban's. "Come on," I said quietly. "Before someone changes their mind."

We walked out together, his height dwarfing mine, the corridor hushed around us. No one stopped us; no one dared. The other alien, Rainse, had given me a wink, unless I'd imagined that. My heart pounded, a drumbeat in my ears. I had no idea what would happen next. I only knew I wasn't going to let Cerban be taken from me and shut away like some dangerous animal.

It took a small eternity to get to his room. I kept expecting someone to step in our way and stop us. He stepped in first, then turned, closing the door behind me. The room was dim, the shutters drawn, the air heavy with salt and his scent. My heart beat against my ribs.

For a moment we just stood there, staring at each other, the silence stretching taut. His gills fluttered once. I dropped my bag on the floor and stepped closer until I could feel the heat of his body radiating through the thin damp fabric of the oversized linen dress I'd put on in a hurry.

"I'm sorry," I whispered, not sure which part I was apologising for – the secrecy, the test, the kiss on the beach. "I didn't mean to make things harder for you."

"You didn't," he said softly. "You saved me."

He lifted a hand and traced his thumb along my cheek, leaving a faint streak of salt water. The touch was so gentle it undid me. All the tension, all the fighting and rules and fear melted away until there was nothing left but this pull between us, tidal and unstoppable.

I licked my lips. "Cerban..."

"Yes?"

"I don't want to talk anymore."

He inhaled sharply, the sound almost a growl. "Then tell me to stop now. Because once I start, Maelis, I won't stop."

I didn't tell him to stop. I closed the space between us and kissed him again.

This time it wasn't tentative. His arms wrapped around me, lifting me off the floor, his mouth deep and sure on mine. The taste of him was salt and heat, the ocean and something entirely his. My fingers slid over his shoulders, over the slick strands of algae trailing from his skin, until I was gripping hard, pulling him closer.

He broke the kiss just enough to look at me. "Are you sure?" he asked, his voice a low rumble against my lips.

"Yes," I breathed. "I've never been surer of anything."

His answering smile was feral and tender all at once. "Then I'll show you what it means when a finman claims his mate."

He kissed me again, slow this time, exploratory, his hands skimming down my back and along my hips until they found the hem of my dress. I shivered as he began to move it up, inch by inch, the cool air meeting my heated skin. He pulled the dress over my head in one smooth motion, leaving me in nothing but damp panties. But I didn't feel self-aware. I just wanted more of him. I pressed against him, feeling the hard planes of his chest through the damp wrap, the way his body trembled as if he were holding himself in check.

"Easy," I whispered. "We have time."

"Not enough," he murmured, kissing down the side of my throat. "But I'll make every moment count."

I arched into him, the last of my defences falling away. The scent of the sea, the sound of his breath, the weight of his hands on my hips – it was all-consuming. For once I wasn't thinking about rules or tests or Pam or the IA. Just us. Just now.

He lifted me easily, carrying me toward the bed, his mouth never leaving mine. When he laid me down, his eyes were dark and bright all at once, like deep water catching the sun. "Maelis," he said again, as if my name was an oath. "Mine."

"Yours," I whispered back, pulling him down to me.

The dim light turned the beads of water on his skin into scattered jewels. I reached up and touched one, letting it roll down my fingertip. He watched me do it, breathing hard, as though that tiny gesture was the most intimate thing in the universe.

"I keep thinking this isn't real," I whispered.

His thumb brushed over my lower lip. "It is," he said. "You're real. We are."

He bent down, kissing me again, slower this time. Everything about him was careful, reverent. The weight of his body pressed into mine, solid and warm, and I could feel the steady rhythm of his heartbeat through his chest.

My fingers slid along his shoulder blades to where skin turned into algae-like sheets. Greenskin, he'd called it.

Gingerly, I traced it, admiring just how smooth and silky it felt.

A low sound rumbled in his throat – not a word, not quite a growl, but something that made heat bloom deep in my stomach. I drew another slow line across his chest. The movement of his greenskin followed me, shimmering faintly in the half-light.

"Maelis…" His voice was rough, strained. "You have no idea what that does to me."

He closed his eyes for a moment, breathing unevenly. "You're touching more than skin," he said. "That's part of me… everything I feel moves through it. And if I didn't know already that you're my mate, the reaction of my greenskin would tell me for sure."

I rose to meet him, our mouths finding each other again, slower and deeper this time. The warmth of his body surrounded me, the rhythm of his breathing matching my own.

His lips left mine only to blaze a path lower, across my jaw, down the line of my throat. Each kiss made me arch, made my pulse pound harder against his mouth. His hands explored me slowly, reverently, as though memorising every inch of bare skin.

I trembled when his mouth reached the swell of my breast. He paused, looking up, giving me the chance to stop him. I didn't. I couldn't. I was already lost to the feeling of him – the heat of his breath, the subtle rasp of his greenskin against my ribs, the way his touch asked for nothing but made me want to give everything.

When his lips finally closed around my nipple, I almost stopped breathing. His tongue circled slowly, deliberately, and something low and helpless escaped my throat.

I curled my fingers into his hair – soft and damp from the sea – and held him close. His mouth was warm, his touch reverent, like I was the first and only woman he'd ever worshipped.

"Cerban..." I whispered, the word barely sound, only need.

He hummed in response, the vibration going straight through me. His greenskin responded to my rising heartbeat, the strands moving like sea-grass in a current, brushing against me as though echoing his intent.

He lingered there, his mouth closing again around my puckered nipple with aching slowness. His tongue teased in lazy circles, coaxing more gasps from my lips, until my back arched of its own accord.

Pleasure coiled low in my belly, sharp and golden. I'd never been touched like this before – not with such focus, such single-minded reverence.

His other hand slid up to cup my other breast, thumb brushing across the sensitive peak as his mouth continued its unhurried worship. I couldn't stay still.

My hips shifted restlessly beneath him, my breath shallow and fast.

"Please," I whispered. I wasn't even sure what I was asking for – more? Less? To stop before I shattered?

He lifted his head, just long enough to look me in the eye. "Tell me what you need," he murmured, voice low and rough as distant surf.

"You," I said. "All of you."

He smiled – all warmth and hunger mixed with sharp teeth – and then he kissed the centre of my chest, just above my pounding heart, before beginning his slow descent.

His mouth moved lower, over the dip of my sternum, along my ribs. The feel of his greenskin brushing my stomach – those living strands shifting with my every breath – made me tremble all over again.

He paused at the waistband of my panties, the barest whisper of his breath making me dizzy. His hands curled around my hips, grounding me as the world tilted. I was ready to come, and he hadn't even touched me down there yet. No man had ever had this effect on me.

He hovered at the edge of my panties, his breath warm against the thin fabric. One of his hands slid down to stroke my hip, the other splaying across my stomach to keep me grounded.

"Tell me to stop," he whispered, his voice a tremor of restraint. "Or tell me to go on."

I couldn't speak. I nodded once, my fingers sliding into his damp hair, urging him lower.

With slow, deliberate movements he hooked his thumbs under the waistband and drew the fabric down, inch by inch, until the last barrier between us was gone. The cool air of the room kissed my newly bared skin, followed immediately by the heat of him – his hands, his breath, the living strands of his greenskin brushing against my thighs like a tide coming in.

He pressed a reverent kiss just above my hip, then another lower, each one a promise. I gasped; my body arched into his touch. He kissed lower, his breath warm and reverent against my skin. My thighs trembled as he settled between them, every brush of his soft lips sending sparks skittering along my nerves.

I gasped when he found my clit – light at first, as though he was still worshipping, still learning the shape of my need. His hands gripped my hips, steadying me, coaxing me open as he traced slow, deliberate paths with his tongue.

The world narrowed to sensation: the heat of his mouth, the pressure building inside me, the way my name sounded when he groaned it softly against me.

Pleasure gathered low in my belly, tidal and consuming. My fingers curled in his hair, holding him there as he unravelled me completely – inch by inch, breath by breath. His tongue did things to me that should not have been possible. I lost myself in the pure, primal pleasure as he guided me to my shattering, and I screamed and begged and screamed for more.

My body bowed beneath him, lost to the rhythm he set – patient, worshipful, unrelenting. He read every sigh, every tremor, as if my pleasure were a language cnly he could speak. When he finally drew back, his lips brushing my inner thigh in a lingering kiss, I reached for him instinctively, not ready for the absence of his mouth.

"Don't stop," I breathed, my voice ragged with wanting.

"Don't worry," he promised. "I'm just getting started."

He got up to his full height and slowly unclasped the leather wrap around his waist. My breath stuttered as I focused on what had been hidden from me until now. I had wondered, admittedly, what a finman cock would look like.

He was... magnificent.

Not like a human. Not at all. His cock was a rich shade of kelp green at the base, deepening toward an oceanic blue at the head, which glistened like wet stone. Thick ridges pulsed just beneath the surface, moving in a wave-like rhythm that made my thighs clench instinctively. That would feel incredible inside me. Below, there were three balls instead of two, their skin smooth and tight, framed by faint lines that reminded me of the ripples left by tidepools.

He curled his fingers around himself with ease, the skin beneath shifting under his touch, almost like it responded to his desire. My mouth went dry.

"I..." I tried to find words, but they scattered like startled fish.

His grin was feral and gentle all at once. "Do you like what you see?"

"You look..." I got to my knees and reached for him, unable to stop myself. "Beautiful."

He shuddered at the touch, the ridges beneath his skin fluttering against my palm.

For just a moment, reason and rationality returned to my feverish mind. "Do you have a condom? Or..."

"There is no risk of pregnancy," he said slowly. "Finboys are given a pill when they reach puberty that makes them sterile until the time they are chosen by the Matriarchs to have a mate. Then the process is reversed with yet another drug. I have not been given it. And I am clean. I won't be passing on anything to you, even if it were possible between our two species."

There was a lot to unpack. And we would, at some point. But not now. I licked my lips, staring at his gorgeous cock. He cupped my face with one broad hand, eyes dark and luminous at the same time.

"Maelis…" he murmured, a warning and a plea all at once.

"I want to taste you," I whispered back, my voice shaking with more than just desire.

For a moment he stayed very still, his thumb brushing my lip as if to anchor himself. Then he let his hand fall away, his body taut with restraint, as I leaned closer, exploring him with my mouth the way I had with my hands – slowly, reverently, like discovering a secret.

He groaned, the sound low and raw, his greenskin shivering beneath my touch as though alive, reacting to every stroke, every breath. My name spilled from his lips in a broken whisper, and the world shrank to the warmth of his body and the taste of salt and ocean on my tongue.

18

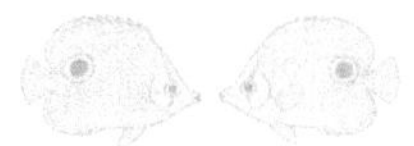

Cerban

She was fire and storm and everything I'd never dared to dream of.

Her lips were soft, reverent, and when she took me into her mouth, I nearly lost the last threads of my control. My hands curled into the blanket beneath me, claws scraping fabric, because if I touched her now, I wouldn't be able to stop. Every instinct inside me clamoured for her – to hold, to claim, to bury myself in her warmth and never let go.

But she didn't need my control. She had power in her every movement – not just the way she touched me, but the way she looked at me, like I wasn't a curiosity or a monster, but something sacred. Desired. Hers.

My vision blurred, the lights of the room fading beneath the riot of sensation building inside me. My skin shimmered beneath her touch, waves of iridescent green flickering across my chest and hips, the algae reacting to her with devotion I couldn't begin to understand.

"Maelis," I breathed, her name breaking from me like prayer. "If you keep... I won't last."

She looked up, her eyes bright with mischief and something far deeper – and then she kissed her way up my body, slow and sure, every brush of her lips setting my soul on fire. When she straddled me, her thighs firm against my hips, her hands resting on my chest, I thought my heart might shatter from the sheer awe of her.

"I want this," she said simply. "I want *you*."

I surged up to meet her, our mouths crashing together – not careful this time, not restrained. This was hunger. Need. The wild, aching drive to become one.

When I finally sank into her, the world split open. She gasped, her fingers digging into my shoulders, and I felt everything – the tight heat of her body, the way her heartbeat stuttered against mine, the pure, radiant rightness of it.

There was no hesitation now. No holding back.

We moved together like the sea and the moon – pulled and pulling, pushing and yielding. My hands gripped her hips, her nails raked down my back, and every roll of her body sent sparks through my veins. She was surrounding me, claiming me, becoming part of me.

And I let her.

With every thrust, every whispered moan, the bond between us deepened – not the kind of bond you needed tests or DNA to prove, but something older, truer. My mate. My heart. My other half.

The climax came like a wave breaking – sudden, immense, all-consuming. She cried out my name as she shuddered above me, and I followed with a roar, my head falling back, arms locking around her as the world tilted and shattered and came back together with her at the centre of it.

When it was over, we lay tangled together, breathless and trembling, hearts still racing in sync.

She lay against me like she'd always belonged there – her skin warm on mine, her breath steady now, soft against my shoulder. I kept my hand on her back, not for comfort, but for reassurance. To remind myself this was real. She was real.

Her fingers moved in slow, aimless shapes along my chest, tracing patterns on my skin. I let my eyes close, drinking in the closeness. The scent of her. The calm after the storm.

It felt like a dream. And maybe it was. I had always dreamed of this, all my life. Having a mate in my arms, mine, utterly mine. For a long time, it had seemed like a dream that could never become true. The Matriarchs had not deemed me worthy of a mate. If it hadn't been for my brother stumbling across the biggest secret of them all, I would still be alone.

"You know, I used to hate aliens," Maelis muttered suddenly. Her voice was hoarse from crying her release.

I opened my eyes but didn't move. Her tone wasn't hostile – more like a confession that had been waiting too long to be spoken.

"Hate is a strong word," I said carefully.

"I know." Her hand stilled, resting just over my heart. "I didn't mean it like that. It wasn't... personal. Just everything that came with you. The changes. This island had been a place for rich people to come and relax. Most of them weren't even interested in diving. They just wanted to sunbathe and eat fancy food and hide from the tax man. I had a lot of free time to do whatever I wanted. When the dating agency took over the ownership of the island, everything changed. Suddenly, we couldn't just be who we were any more – we had to make space for you. For all of you."

She paused, then let out a humourless laugh. "And the dating stuff? Don't get me started. Humans falling over themselves for a chance to match with an alien. I didn't like seeing it. I always felt like some of those girls didn't know any better. They were so desperate to find their true love that they would take anyone - including aliens."

I turned my head to study her face, half-hidden against me. There was no malice there. Just honesty. Tired honesty.

"Did you ever see a match go wrong?" I asked gently. "Was there ever a human woman who was unhappy with the alien she'd been matched with?"

Maelis thought for a moment. "No. I don't think so. They were all besotted with each other. But that was partly what infuriated me. It looked so easy. For them. Why was it so hard for me to find someone? And I think that's why I stopped looking. I didn't want to be disappointed."

"And you never applied to the dating agency."

She laughed. "I most certainly didn't. Until today. Part of me thinks that I should have doubts. That I should wait until we have the DNA results. But... humans fall in love all the time without scientific tests to confirm their love. Why should it be different for us?"

"Love... Say it again." I needed her to say it.

Maelis looked me straight in the eyes. "I love you."

I leaned down and kissed her, not out of hunger or heat, but something deeper. Gratitude. Devotion. Relief.

And then her stomach rumbled.

She groaned. I laughed.

"You're hungry," I said, pressing a kiss to her cheek.

"I'm starving," she grumbled. "But if you even suggest seaweed–"

"Never." I grinned. "For you, only the finest dry land cuisine. Something crispy. Perhaps... those plant things Rainse discovered."

"Plant things? You'll have to be more specific."

"Yellow slices of something that is a little sweet and very starchy. I've had them salted and dipped in a sweet sticky liquid."

"Plantain!" She laughed. "Gods, I could kiss you again just for that."

"Then I insist you do."

And she did.

19

Maelis

I'd lost track of time in Cerban's room. Days passed in a flash.

We talked for hours, about everything and nothing. About diving, about the places I'd lived and travelled to, about his childhood in the kelp gardens of Finfolkaheem, growing up with Fionn and Rainse. We listened to music, switching between my old playlists and Cerban's favourites that reminded me of whale song mixed with techno beats.

At some point, I'd played *Stand Up* again, the way I had the day everything changed. The moment the first chords filled the air, Cerban froze. Then he reached for my hand.

"Your song," he murmured. "The one that called to me."

We didn't speak for the rest of it – we just listened. And when the final notes faded, he kissed me so tenderly it made my ribs ache.

There had been a lot of kissing after that. And more. A whole lot more.

We didn't leave the room except to grab food or take hurried showers. The staff turned a blind eye. Rainse checked on us under the pretence of bringing us snacks. Tyrone winked the one time we passed him in the corridor.

I didn't care. Let them gossip. Let them speculate. I'd almost drowned. I'd touched an ancient memory orb at the bottom of the sea. I was sleeping with a green-skinned alien who smelled faintly of the tide and kissed like he was made for me.

The world could wait.

But eventually, reality caught up.

Paul came to our door, looking relaxed for the first time in a while. He announced that Finn and Elise had returned on the Tidebound, and they hadn't come alone. Pam was with them. Neither Cerban nor me had ever met her in person before. That had to mean that our test results were back. He left us to get ready, smirking at that as if it was a joke. And maybe it was. We both needed a shower.

Cerban was pacing, his long strides eating up the room. "They would have said something if it was bad," I said, watching him from the bed while brushing my hair. "Right?"

"I do not know how your people operate," he muttered. "Sometimes you like to be cruel in person."

I snorted. "That's fair."

He stopped and turned toward me, his expression serious. "What if it says we're not matched?"

My stomach dipped. We hadn't talked about that. Not properly.

I slid off the bed and crossed to him, wrapping my arms around his waist. "Then we tell them the test is wrong," I said into his chest. "Because I've never felt this way about anyone before. Not even close."

He lowered his head, his mouth brushing my hair. "Nor have I."

A soft knock at the door made us both jump.

"Time to go," Rainse called. "The others are waiting in the conference room."

Cerban sighed, then looked down at me. "Ready, little fish?"

I reached up and kissed him, slow and deliberate. "Let's find out what fate has to say about us."

Fionn and Elise were already seated. She smiled when she saw me, warm and familiar, her hand resting lightly over his. I remembered briefly meeting her weeks ago, back when I still thought aliens were something to be endured, not trusted.

Now I was walking into a room with a finman's hand tightly curled around mine.

Pam sat at the head of the table, tablet in hand. Her expression was unreadable – that calm, efficient mask she wore when things were about to get serious. Paul stood beside her, arms folded.

"Take a seat," Pam said, gesturing to the two empty chairs across from her.

Cerban and I sat down. Our fingers remained laced together beneath the table.

Pam didn't waste time. "Three days ago, I received a call informing me that a certain finman had broken confinement and a human diver had disappeared again. I was fully prepared to authorise a full withdrawal of the finfolk delegation. It was all becoming too unpredictable and risky."

Cerban stiffened beside me. I squeezed his hand.

"But," Pam continued, "sometimes things are a little different than I first thought. After years of working with alien species, I shouldn't be surprised any more, really, but... well, I suppose it's a good thing that life is full of surprises. It keeps me young."

"I wish," Paul muttered. "I think I've aged by ten years this week."

"Don't be silly, you're still gorgeous as ever," Pam chuckled. For a moment, I wondered if the two of them had something going on. But no, Pam would be on the island much more often if that was the case.

Pam focused back on Cerban and me. "Anyway, I fast tracked your DNA sample, and it has been added to the Hot Tatties database. I'm pleased to say there has been a match."

I knew the match was to Cerban. There was no doubt in my mind about it. But then why was my heart beating fast and my breathing shallow?

Pam smiled widely. "Don't worry. I won't prolong this any further. The two of you are a match. With all the accuracy that the Hot Tatties algorithm allows - and I'd like to point out that it has never failed - I can announce that Cerban Arken-Clutch of Eynhallow and Maelis Jane Prescod have officially been matched."

I felt like this was a moment to applaud, but I kept my hands steady.

"That means that we now have four official matches between humans and finfolk," Pam continued. "Fionn, Pli'th, Hournn and Cerban. Considering barely more than twenty finmen came to Earth, that is a very good ratio in my opinion. I have to admit, I was a bit sceptical in the beginning whether we'd be able to find any matches for you. It's the same every time a new alien species contacts me. They are always full of hope, but it doesn't always work out in the end."

"During our most recent excursion to the underwater cave-" Cerban began, but Paul interrupted him, his eyebrows drawn up.

"Unsanctioned excursion."

I rolled my eyes, but Cerban stayed polite and simply smiled. "Yes. During our unsanctioned excursion, we found further evidence that humans and finfolk have lived together in the past. The stories we heard of Ma'vel and Jonet were not an isolated relationship. Generations ago, when finfolk swam in this planet's oceans, we did more than just inspire legends and tales. We found mates among humans. We even had offspring."

"Cerban is right," I added. "We saw a recording of a girl who looked like a human-finfolk hybrid. I would like to return to the cave to see what other mysteries that alien tech contains. I think we will be able to learn much from it. About ourselves. Our past. And maybe our future."

Pam studied me closely. "Could you bring this alien artefact to the surface?"

Cerban shook his head. "I don't think so. It is part of the cave, an organic mix between technology and nature. I imagine it may have been a sacred place of our ancestors, where they went to retrieve or record memories of their lives."

"It would be curious to know what knowledge is contained in there. Maybe it will help us find more matches for your kind." Pam pursed her lips. "Alright. I'm putting the two of you in charge of that project. You will have to record everything you see and find down there. And I need you to make it safe. No more near misses. No more cave collapses. And if a finman even so much thinks that there may be a storm coming, it is his responsibility to tell the humans on this island."

"I will make sure of that personally," Fionn said, speaking for the first time. "The Tidebound's systems have advanced weather detection features. Whenever the ship is on the island, we will pass on anything of interest to Paul and the other resort staff. I feel like we have been guests here so far. I would love to be able to say that we are more than that - in future."

Pam smiled. "We will discuss that further in private. The agency is planning to use this island for future alien-human introductions, but there is another large private island up for sale not far from here. Maybe that could become a home for the finmen who want to stay."

"And their mates," Elise said. "Fionn and I realised during our trip to Scotland that it would be impossible for us to live in a normal town or city, even a village. Fionn can't stay at home permanently, hiding from everyone. We have talked about moving to Finfolkaheem, but as much as I love swimming, I'm not sure I could handle living underwater for such prolonged periods of time. We need an alternative."

I listened with interest. Cerban and I hadn't really talked about our future much, at least not the practical aspects. I would love to see his planet, see the world that he'd described to me, dive in its waters - but living there? I wasn't so sure about that. An island where humans and finfolk could live together, close to the sea yet with buildings on land, sounded perfect.

After the meeting, Fionn and Elise waited for us outside the room. Elise and I hugged, and I remembered how I'd taken her on that fateful dive during which Kelon had abducted her. Both of us had experienced much in the depths beneath the island - and both had found our mates down there.

"Congratulations," Elise cheered. "I know there are two other finmen with human mates, but they haven't met their matches yet. You two are therefore the second official couple. I'm glad Fionn and I are no longer alone."

Fionn extended a hand to me and I shook it. He'd clearly taken lessons in human behaviour. "Welcome to the family, Maelis. I'm sorry we weren't there during these tumultuous days. It seems my brother has drawn the ire of the entire island."

I laughed. "He also saved my life. And he showed me that aliens aren't all that bad after all."

Elise rolled her shoulders. "It's been a long day. How about a swim?"

20

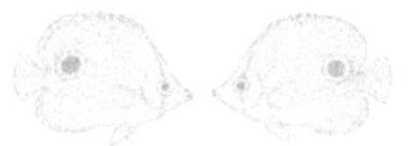

Maelis

The sea welcomed us like an old friend.

We slipped beneath the surface just after sunrise, the horizon kissed with gold and coral-pink light. The water was calm, visibility near-perfect – as though the ocean itself approved of our return.

Cerban swam beside me, long and graceful, his presence a comforting weight in the water. His warm hand brushed mine briefly before he surged ahead, leading the way through the familiar reef shallows, then deeper, into the crevasse that had nearly become my grave.

But fear didn't follow me this time. Only wonder.

We both carried extra tanks, fresh lights, and a compact data recorder given to us by Fionn, which would sync everything we recorded with the Tidebound's computer. It was our first trip to the memory orb in our new roles - and it felt strange not having to sneak out in secret.

We knew the way now. Past the fractured rockfall, through the narrow side channel revealed only by that curious stream of bubbles. The entrance glowed faintly as we approached, the shimmer of veins in the stone like a heartbeat just beneath the surface.

Cerban reached for the orb, his hand tracing the same figure-eight pattern he'd used last time. The sphere awoke slowly – light flaring in gentle pulses, the water around us vibrating softly.

A bubble formed around the orb, then began to expand.

I sank to the floor as the air displaced the water, feeling the now-familiar sensation of weightlessness turn to grounded stillness. My mask hissed as I pulled it free, heart pounding with anticipation.

Cerban straightened beside me, water rolling off his skin. He looked radiant in the shifting glow – all sharp lines and sea-worn grace, his emerald skin glistening like kelp in sunlight.

"This place remembers us," he said quietly. "It was much faster this time."

"I was just thinking the same thing."

Cerban reached for the data recorder and pointed it at the orb. While he did that, I used my waterproof camera to film the cave in all its detail. We didn't speak for a while. Just moved together in easy rhythm, documenting what we could. The orb pulsed steadily, as if listening.

"I think I've got everything I can for now," Cerban said eventually. "Let's activate the orb and see what else it might show us. Are you ready?"

I pointed the camera straight at the sphere. "Ready."

There were small images at first. A child's laughter. A pair of hands building something intricate from coral. The ghost of a kiss exchanged beneath glowing water. Just fragments of past memories, yet significant, nonetheless.

I turned to Cerban, breath caught in my throat. "It's showing us other things than last time."

He nodded. "I don't know how to control what it shows us. Maybe someone on the Tidebound will know. For now, I think it's best if we just watch and record everything."

One of the projections showed a gathering – dozens of finfolk and humans seated together in a circle, exchanging objects. Gifts? Tools? Promises? Either way, it was proof yet again that there had been a true relationship between our two species, long ago, before the finfolk had returned to their planet.

The recorder captured everything, but I didn't look away from the images. I couldn't. This was no longer just discovery – it was legacy. A shared past stretching far deeper than any of us had realised.

"I want to learn everything," I whispered. "I want to know what they built together. What they lost. What we can find again."

Cerban took my hand. "Then we will. Together."

I looked around the glowing chamber – at the veins of light, the hum that resonated in my bones, the quiet certainty that we were meant to find this.

Maybe the sea hadn't almost taken me that day in the cave.

Maybe it had chosen to let me in.

And maybe... just maybe... this was only the beginning.

I pulled Cerban closer. "I am so glad I get to share this with you. Thank you for saving me that day."

"I saved you from drowning, but you saved me from a life without love," he muttered.

He stared into my eyes, but then his gaze flickered to something behind me, distracted. I turned to see a new memory, a finwoman and a human man dancing in slow, elegant motions.

We exchanged a look. Cerban began to hum a melody.

I recognised it from the very first notes. *Stand up*. He remembered.

And so, we danced, our very first dance together, in the cave that held our past, our present, our future.

# EPILOGUE

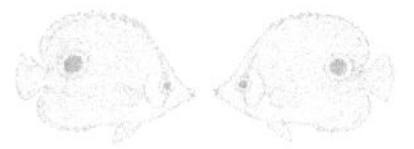

Verity

I'd always loved whales. Until the day one tried to kill me.

Or maybe it didn't. Maybe it just wanted to play and didn't consider that it was so much bigger than the RIB.

Either way, it hit us like a truck, slamming into the boat from the side. The impact tore through the inflatable's hull with a sound like thunder. There was no time to radio for help. We were in the water before we could blink.

One moment, we were laughing about the playlist Hugo had put on – *Under the Sea*, of all things – and the next, the world flipped upside down. Cold swallowed me whole. The sea punched the air from my lungs, and I barely remembered to close my mouth before the saltwater rushed in. My life jacket yanked me upwards, forcing me to the surface just in time to see the whale's tail fin rise like a mountain behind me, then crash down, sending a wave that rolled me over again.

When I surfaced a second time, coughing and choking, it was gone. Its work was done.

The sea around us was a chaos of foam and debris. The overturned RIB bobbed nearby, half-submerged. The engine hissed and spat before dying entirely.

"Hugo!" I gasped, throat raw from salt and panic.

He surfaced a few metres away, eyes wide, coughing up seawater. "I'm here! Jammie?"

A spluttered reply came from somewhere to my left. Relief, sharp and fleeting. All three of us. Alive. For now.

We tried to stay afloat as the sea rocked us like rag dolls. There was nothing around us but endless blue – no shore, no boats, no sign of rescue. The Minerva, our main vessel, had to be out there somewhere, but the swell made it impossible to spot her. The horizon was a jagged line between sea and sky.

I tilted my head back and stared at the sky. A single gull circled high above us, its cry thin and lonely. The world was too vast, too silent, too indifferent.

I'd always loved whales. Their songs, their grace, their impossible size. It's why I had spent my adult life studying them. But floating there, tiny and breakable in the endless ocean, I realised love could be as dangerous as it was beautiful.

Now, we could only wait to be rescued.

Or to become part of the deep.

*Maelis and Cerban got their happily ever after, but will marine biologist Verity find her finman? Find out in* **Rainse***, the third book in the Starlight Mermen. New to the series? Start with* **Fionn***.*

*Want to know more about Ma'vel and Jonet, the couple whose union was described in the Archives? Read the prequel to the series, Ma'vel, set in 17th century Scotland, for free!*
**skyemackinnon.com/mavel**

*The Hot Tatties Dating Agency has many clients... meet some hunky alien Highlanders in the* Starlight Highlanders *and honourable Norsemen in the* Starlight Vikings*!*

THE STARLIGHT UNIVERSE

*This book is part of the Starlight Universe, an entire galaxy filled with hunky aliens, exotic planets, and the human women ready to find love among the stars.*

## Starlight Highlanders Mail Order Brides

Alien Highlanders in kilts come to Earth in search of brides... and take them to planet Albya. Three m/f standalones full of humour, action and steamy romance. Part of the Intergalactic Dating Agency.

## Starlight Vikings

Set on Earth and on the spaceship Valkyr, this trilogy of m/f standalones is all about hunky alien Vikings in need of females. Part of the Intergalactic Dating Agency.

## Starlight Mermen

Hundreds of years ago, they crash-landed on Earth and gave rise to many of our legends. Now, they're back, desperate for female mates. Part of the Intergalactic Dating Agency.

## The Intergalactic Guide to Humans

A humorous take on alien abductions, probing and other shenanigans. One reverse harem trilogy about clueless aliens and the human woman they abducted, followed by several standalone romances with various pairings (m/f, f/m/f and m/m). If you want light entertainment filled with unicorns, fabulous misunderstandings and unusual body parts, this is the series for you.

## Starlight Monsters

These aliens are not your usual humanoids... they have claws, fangs, tails, scales, knotty dicks and will growl at you. Interconnected m/f standalones with lots of action, steam and fated mates.

# ABOUT THE AUTHOR

Skye MacKinnon is a Scottish romance author who was raised by elves in the mystical Highlands and calls the Loch Ness monster her friend. Her bestselling books weave together romance with action, suspense and whimsical humour, creating page-turners filled with strong heroines, alpha heroes and loveable monsters.

Whether she's writing about aliens in kilts, hunky Vikings or cat shifter assassins, Skye likes to put a new spin on familiar tropes. Some of her heroines don't have to choose, some fall in love with other women, and others get abducted by clueless aliens.

Skye lives with her bossy cat on the west coast of Scotland and uses the dramatic views from her office as an inspiration, no matter whether she writes fantasy, paranormal or science fiction romance. Until she gets abducted by aliens, that is.

Subscribe to her newsletter:
**skyemackinnon.com/newsletter**

# ALSO BY

Find all of Skye's books on her website,
**skyemackinnon.com**, where you can also order signed
paperbacks and swag.

Many of her books are available as audiobooks.

Science Fiction Romance

**Set in the Starlight Universe**

- **Starlight Vikings** (sci-fi m/f romance)
- **Starlight Mermen** (sci-fi m/f romance)
- **Starlight Monsters** (sci-fi m/f romance)
- **Starlight Highlanders Mail Order Brides**
  (sci-fi m/f romance)
- **The Intergalactic Guide to Humans** (sci-fi
  romance with various pairings)

**Set in other worlds**

- **Between Rebels** (sci-fi reverse harem set in the Planet Athion shared world)
- **The Mars Diaries** (sci-fi reverse harem)
- **Aliens and Animals** (f/f sci-fi romance co-written with Arizona Tape)

## Paranormal & Fantasy Romance

- **Claiming Her Bears** (post-apocalyptic shifter reverse harem)
- **Daughter of Winter** (fantasy reverse harem)
- **Catnip Assassins** (urban fantasy reverse harem)
- **Infernal Descent** (paranormal reverse harem based on Dante's Inferno, co-written with Bea Paige)
- **Seven Wardens** (fantasy reverse harem co-written with Laura Greenwood)
- **The Lost Siren** (post-apocalyptic, paranormal reverse harem co-written with Liza Street)

## Other Series

- **Academy of Time** (time travel academy standalones, reverse harem and m/f)
- **Defiance** (contemporary reverse harem with a hint of thriller/suspense)

## Standalones

- Song of Souls – m/f fantasy romance, fairy tale retelling
- Highland Butterflies – sapphic romance
- Wings of Time and Fate - epic fantasy

## Box Sets

- Daggers & Destiny – a fantasy romance starter library
- Stars & Seduction - a science fiction romance starter library